LETTERS TO A YOUNG POLITICIAN

'The PM has just rung me, he hears there is to be a leadership challenge. Do I by chance know whom his opponents have chosen as their candidate? Could it by chance be the Chairman of the Party? I doubt it, I reply, but why not ask him to propose you, that will smoke him out. The PM likes this idea. I must say, this man knows how to plot. I cannot conceive of him staying in power, but the Party are now about to engage in the only activity at which he excels.'

A stylish and compelling fable of scandal, ambition and character assassination in the treacherous world of politics. Written in the form of letters sent from a senior party apparatchik to his young nephew, *Letters to a Young Politician* follows the career of a typically ruthless MP as he rises through the ranks as backbencher and junior minister. The fascination of the book lies in the developing relationship between cynical Uncle and ambitious Nephew. Alistair McAlpine, former Treasurer and Deputy Chairman of the Conservative Party, has written another remarkable study of the inescapably treacherous and reckless nature of political life.

Lord McAlpine was Treasurer of the Conservative Party from 1975 to 1990 and Deputy Chairman from 1979 to 1983, and now writes for the *Spectator*, *Sunday Express* and the *European*. He is the author of *The Servant*.

Letters
to a Young Politician

From his Uncle

ALISTAIR MCALPINE

faber and faber
LONDON · BOSTON

First published in 1995
by Faber and Faber Limited
3 Queen Square London WC1N 3AU
This paperback edition first published in 1996

Photoset by Intype London Ltd.
Printed in England by Clays Ltd, St Ives plc

A CIP record for this book
is available from the British Library

ISBN 0-571-17756-5

2 4 6 8 10 9 7 5 3 1

To F.B. and D.B.,
whom I hold in the highest regard

Letters
to a Young Politician

Dear Nephew

It was a pleasure to see you on Thursday afternoon. I enjoyed our conversation, news of your mother and your sisters – riveting stuff. And as for the originality of your ideas, I came away convinced that you were a well brought up young man, eminently suited for the heartland of British mediocrity.

No doubt you will in time become a great figure and run the institutions of our nation. Climb with all the skill of those without imagination to a position of power and influence – always fair, always a mediator, finding that middle way which in truth helps none but yourself, careful never to offend or oppose those in power, never hesitating to step on the heads of those who show originality, courage and imagination, striking them at the moment that they are weak. Cutting the throats only of those who have them located at the back of their necks.

A man hopping from one position of power to a greater one, a man whose brain has no connection with his spine. A man of iron who will never be influenced by justice or honour. An intelligent man who realizes that his future lies not with principles but with how men regard him. You may even learn to become a man meticulous in the matter of manners, never impolite without a reason.

Nephew, let me remind you that on Thursday I spent time with you, a valuable commodity at least as far as I am concerned. This seems to be of little consequence to you. I have received no call, no note of thanks, not a single word. I took you out to tea, but perhaps you thought that I should have given you dinner complete with a good claret, cigar and Armagnac? It is customary to write a letter of thanks when a person has taken trouble and expense on your behalf – and

[3]

bored me almost to death with your half-learned philosophies. If you must steal from great men and women, at least do them the credit of purloining with accuracy. You might even attribute their ideas; it at least shows that you have an education, if not a mind.

Nephew, you were downright rude in your behaviour to me, and that, my dear boy, is the only aspect of hope that I find in the whole of you. Practise rudeness, take it, polish it, turn it into an art, and in time, because of your talent for rudeness, you may become much favoured. I will write to you from time to time, and it may be that I can tell you of matters that in the natural course of events would take you years to learn. I will do this because my sister, your mother, asks it of me. I owe it to her for she has been to me wife, mother and family.

My life has been a lonely one, watching mankind at work or pretending to join it in pleasure. Always remember that the course you set out on is a single course, it must become both your work and your pleasure. Whatever you would achieve, it must be a part of you, there must be no question of choice in how a day is filled. If you have any hesitation in this matter, give up now, go to Cirencester and study farming, rather than Oxford and then to politics.

You wish to enter politics? I strongly advise you against it, for in the public's eye it is a profession worse regarded than breaking and entering. You will become fair game for the Press, and for any creature who chooses to blackmail you. You will become the butt of humour on television. Vile accusations will be made to your face across the dinner table, and worse still, when people listen with reverence to what you tell them, then you will know in your heart that you are failing. Abuse and brickbats will be your daily fare, and you will dismiss this as rubbish, as at best the distorted sense of humour of your friends the Press. But when the same men praise you, you will regard them as sage critics. In the end you will read nothing and listen to little, myopically fixing your mind on some small achievement, for government is an act of choosing between several alternatives, none of which really appeals to you. Long before you reach office the barnacles of abuse will accumulate on your soul, giving it a skin hard to penetrate, painful to brush against.

If you would truly achieve the goal that you say is your reason for starting on this career in politics, you must follow a lonely course. You will be tempted – perhaps already I have tempted you, I have shown you the way to easy privilege and fortune, even to temporary fame. That way, however, leads to history's rubbish tip, a place in the volumes of names. No, you say you will set out in the world of politics fixedly determined to make your 'mark' on our society. If you are to succeed, you cannot be, as many of your contemporaries will turn out to be, a man of convenience, your actions bought by position or title, taking the former for the benefit of your family and the latter for the benefit of your wife. You, Nephew, must be a man apart, and that is why I remark on your rudeness.

First, in a man who would climb the political ladder it is unexpected. Secondly, it makes others treat you with caution, never knowing how their words will be received.

Nephew, next week you go up to Oxford. This is a time to learn. Learn the history of politics – this can be useful in argument. But, more important, learn about the theatre. Learn how to deliver words so that others will not only hear them but will listen to them, and remember them. At the Union you will learn the art of debate. The theatre, however, will teach you the quality of words.

Dear boy, please give my love and affection to your mother – your father I see often enough in Westminster, and as you know I have neither love nor affection for him. Under no circumstances try to follow in your father's footsteps. Rather the reverse should be the case. I will talk of him when I next write.

Your Uncle

PS I will write as and when I should. These letters need no reply, burn them or read them as you like.

Dear Nephew

I have just finished a rather tiresome conversation with your father. Most conversations with him tend to be tiresome, and on this particular occasion he excelled himself. He has not an original idea in his head, yet he lectures me on success. Deputy chairman of a joint stock bank, the boards of fourteen other companies, what a success! A worthy of the Twenty-two Committee – sixteen years on its executive, a perennial of the back benches, flowering only when hanging and Sunday trading are debated, voting for the former and against the latter.

You should just hear him ask those set-piece questions of the Prime Minister at question time. He gracefully tosses them into the Chamber, and smiles respectfully when the Prime Minister knocks them for six. Your father is always the voice of that tiresome creature sweet reason – sweet enough to make you vomit and so reasonable that a man can be driven to violence by its logic. Wrong, totally and unutterably wrong. And now your father is involving himself in the matter of your career, for your mother has told him of our tea-time rendezvous.

Dear boy, I must tell you before he does that you would be wrong to take my advice – on this your father and I agree. Wrong but courageous. With an uncertain future ahead, you will have a chance to wrestle with opportunity, fight ill fortune, in time to have that greatest of all achievements, to be your own man. This, my Nephew, is where your father and I differ. Your father believes that he too has known all of these things. He feels that after twenty-five years on the back benches he is exactly that – his own man. Far from it. What he puts forward as a model for your future is his past: corrupt and always second-rate. Eight times he has stood at the polls and been elected. Twice before that, the people of the constituency where he stood had the good sense to send him packing. Eight times he has supported a manifesto that he had no part in drawing up, indeed he had sometimes seen only a week or two before Polling Day. He has seen pledges that he endorsed changed, after only the smallest amount of discussion. Often he has trooped through the lobbies of the Commons voting for what must conflict not only with his conscience but with his direct promise to his constituents.

He has spoken out often enough in private, kept silent in public, supposing this behaviour to be virtuous, acting in the interest of the Party, sometimes, he would claim, of the nation. This behaviour has formed his character, and his great talent is his reliability: his reliability to behave within the parameters of his character. This very character has become his reference, the reference that the Bank needed before they gave him his position, complete with all the trappings of car, office and functionaries to carry out his bidding – but far more, they gave him his authority to talk of money and finance as though he knew of these things. Your father has become a sage in these matters. Your father, whose only previous experience of money was the mishandling of your mother's, that and the spending of it on fancy women. The real reason, may I say, that he has assiduously kept to the back benches, is that he dare not venture upwards: he feels terror at the thought that he might fall, and so he sanctifies his position with all the trappings that clever men use to pay fools for compliance. He was made a member of the Privy Council for selling Britain – not Britain's industry, no, not a reward for exports – no, for selling Britain bound heart and soul in a lousy treaty, so squalid its name is barely spoken today except in place of a curse. A fine man, your father, known to have influence. The Bank is happy with his steady presence on the boards of other companies; those companies who would use him to speak to the Bank appoint him to their boards. He could be helpful, they say, both Bank and companies misunderstanding the other's purpose. A steady man – do these practitioners of commerce not see that your father has all the steadiness of a rabbit as it stands, its eyes transfixed by the gaze of a stoat? He finds compromise easy, not because he feels that compromise is right but because he has no alternative, for he fears all but the middle of the road; like a thousand other politicians of his ilk, he stands there while the traffic swerves, leaving him unscathed, but destroying those of thought and imagination who pass by that way. His grey mediocrity is his armour: there is little point in destroying him, so no one tries.

Your father sits on boards and brings the wisdom of industry to waiting politicians, and they, poor dears, listen and are amazed, for they know nothing of commerce. Your father is physically brave, but a moral coward. A man's ability to be morally courageous can vary according to how much is at stake. Like a waiter carrying a tray of empty glasses, he whistles and swings the tray, moving swiftly, for he has little to lose but the glasses. Fill them, however, and much is at risk: then he moves slowly, with care, in silence. A man of influence, that is how your father is perceived, and twice a year he demonstrates his inside information. This is a trick, a cheap little trick, it seems to me.

Nephew, I will tell you his trick, but not so that you can use it yourself – you are destined to a life far beyond an existence on the back benches. No, I tell you so that you can expose those who do use it. Your father sits on the board of a newspaper – you probably read it, I know your mother does. Well, in order that the newspapers can publish the honours lists on the day that they are announced, they are given to newspapers two or three days before that date, with an embargo on their contents. Now, great secrecy surrounds these honours: those who receive them are sworn to say nothing on pain of losing their reward; some don't even tell their wives.

They go about their business for several weeks before the list is published in fear and trembling lest, by accident, their inclusion is known. Well, the more important of them your father calls the moment he sees the list. His conversation goes like this: 'Wonderful, quite wonderful, we tried to get you something better – in time, in time, but for now a knighthood.' The victim of this trick is terrified that his secret is known but impressed beyond measure by your father's power and importance.

These are not the tricks for you, my Nephew. You have to learn many things, but these devices are not those you must study. Your father has strong views on how you should get a seat. I mention this only to show the folly and the conceit of the man. He wants you to take over his constituency, but now is not the time for considering this. When that time comes you must make your own way or you are nothing.

The food in Oxford has greatly improved since I was last there. I cannot say the same for the traffic. The Pitt Rivers Museum was, as always, wonderful. Now there was a great man, Pitt Rivers, a legend amongst collectors. Why don't you give up this political nonsense and become an anthropologist, a traveller, a collector perhaps? In time you could find fame, and perhaps with luck even fortune.

Your Uncle

Dear Nephew

The Square has become a hive of activity. Talk of a snap election fills the corridors. For my money, I doubt very much whether there will be one.

This prime minister seems gripped by indecision. He follows his Cabinet and they, without realizing it, follow each other. Like a party of pig farmers with their pigs on a ferry, one moves to the right-hand side of the boat, they all move, and then, fearing the ferry will capsize, they all move back again, with much the same result. This prime minister is worthy of study, he is the model of all that you should shun. He seems nice, a word I dislike; nice, however, is a word that might have been created with him in mind, for it exactly describes how he seems. I say 'seems' for, as he tries to please all, he must be as confused as everyone else about what he truly feels. When you disagree with him he will, with great patience, explain that he agrees with your aims, but just has to go about things in a different way. 'Trust me' are his favourite words, and as he is such a nice man, many do – to their cost, for in reality the man has not the slightest idea in which direction he is heading. His aims and ambitions, such as they are, are based on petty hatreds and small jealousies accumulated during a career of pulling his forelock to whoever would promote him. All the while he was secretly hedging his bets, keeping company with those who plot and plan, not realizing that there are men who do this for the pure pleasure of it. And this man became prime minister.

And so, dear boy, I am plunged into a pre-election campaign. Confusing, eh? Well, I do not know what it is doing to our opponents, but it has everyone here spinning like tops, and all the while the costs spiral upwards, away into the stratosphere. I doubt if we shall truly recover from this confusion of philosophy, let alone the Party's extravagance, for at least a generation. When our party in government ceases to behave like the party which by tradition it is – then we make no friends, win no elections and generally go broke. The future does not bode well for the likes of me.

I believe that we shall win, not because we deserve to (nor, may I say, do the others deserve to), but because we have a majority at the moment the like of which has never been overturned at one election. Your father, it seems, is in for another five years, and I will have to put up with him. You will learn that it is a rule of politics that those whom you call your friends will study what you feel you deserve and helpfully ensure that you do not obtain it, making certain that you are given only a position you do not want.

Now is the time for thought. Watch, examine, come to your own conclusions, lay the foundations for future achievement. Your father would have you work in Party Headquarters, but that is out of the question. Humility is the lesson for this election, and when it comes, work in a hopeless seat. Politics is about conversion, moving opinions. Study that which changes men's minds, practise on minds that have not changed for generations.

How good of you to invite me to tea at Castello's. I cannot come, for two reasons: first, I hate the place, and second, I am far too busy with the Prime Minister. Give my love to your mother and tell your elder sister that I saw her picture on the front page of *Country Life*. It did not seem to me much of an advertisement for her. She could do with losing a good deal of weight, and as for her letter pointing out the date of her birthday, I would be more inclined to remember hers if she had not forgotten mine.

Your Uncle

Dear Nephew

I must be direct with you. Your criticism of Jermyn's Tea Rooms I feel to be totally unjustified. I have long enjoyed eating there. The food they serve I have always found adequate, that they have no licence an advantage.

While at moments in my life I have found the rhythm of drink at lunch-time and sleep in the afternoon highly pleasurable, I must tell you that such a regime is suitable only for a life of pleasure. There is no profit in it. To drink too much makes your jokes humorous only to yourself, your drunken platitudes make you feel wise, but not seem so. Any emotion, any intelligence that can be found only by nurturing it with alcohol is best kept hidden. The danger of alcohol is – and this you must fully understand – that when you drink with a man his judgement is as distorted as your own. When you joke, he laughs, and so your prejudice to be entertained by your own humour is reinforced. When you pass on to him some piece of wisdom, he finds your words as wise as you believe them to be – and so, day by day, drink by drink, you have an endorsement of your wit and wisdom and you become a fool. Knowing this, you seek the amusing sage that you are after a few drinks, and find that state by having a few more drinks. Then, my dear Nephew, you find you prosper only in the company of other drunks. Nephew, if you must drink, do it only in the company of those for whose opinions you have contempt, so that whether they laugh or praise you or curse you is a matter of complete indifference to you.

Nephew, if you, like me, cannot stand the company of drink-sodden fools, then you must find a drinking companion. Such men are rare. They pay their way, drinking in silence, thinking their own thoughts, leaving you to think yours. When they speak it is only to offer another drink or suggest another place to drink at. These invaluable companions go at the right moment, making no more demand upon you than for help into a taxi.

Take my advice, Nephew, drink if you must but drink for your own purpose. Do not imagine that by taking a man to one of the city's fine restaurants and filling him with expensive wine you will achieve more than a bill longer than you can afford. When you serve wine, serve the best, but always be slightly less than liberal in serving it. Let the food that you serve be perfect but modest in quantity, for a man who has lunched well with you will always return, and men who know that you serve good wine and have your food well cooked will always accept your invitation. Never take the trouble to explain a difficult proposition to your guest and then give him so much wine that he remembers little of what you were telling him. When you dine for companionship, let it be the conversation that excites; that is a stimulant, properly applied, worth the contents of all the cellars in Burgundy. Eat little, drink little, and talk late into the night; never, my Nephew, speak when you cannot properly hear your own words, never be ashamed of what you have said, never wake the next morning wondering what words you used the night before: a full belly dulls the mind. Never mix your pleasures, my Nephew, if you are to succeed, and I believe that, given the right advice, you may – that, I might add, is why I write to you. Should I tell you of my holidays, or ask after your mother, my sister, or, curse him, your father, it is only out of politeness. My pen skips along these lines unconnected to my mind.

No, Nephew, my words may seem frivolous, but it is the frivolous act that has brought down many a great man, or diverted him from the path of greatness. I recall one, I knew him well, who in his cups turned left to his sometime mistress rather than right to his family home. He began again an affair – far better that he had drunk till he fell from the table where

[14]

he dined, but that night he dined with fools and we fed on each other's folly. The trivial seemed of importance, the most important trivial; we drank too much but not enough; we rose to conquer the world; answers, we had them all. All we lacked was a guest capable of asking a half-intelligent question, so, filled with conceit, we set out into the night. The months passed, the prestige of my friend increased, and a child grew in the belly of the woman whom he had known and left. Then, at his hour of triumph, the events of that or some similar night exposed him, left him weakened, and his enemies pulled him down. His enemies come from among the ranks of his friends, my Nephew: it is from the ranks of your friends that your greatest enemies come. Remember that when you drink with friends and tell the secrets of your soul. In sadness he stood before his party at their conference. They sat silent, guilty of their role, three thousand of them sat in judgement on him. I was in the hall, and the irony was that it felt as though they met before a wedding, as if they waited for a bride: they laughed with guilty laughter, they joked with guilty jokes, and as he climbed to the platform they sat silent as though he climbed the gallows. They listened in silence, their applause was polite, they hanged his career on a gibbet of restraint. His friends told him that he was safe, his enemies told all that he should go. That night it hung in the balance. I watched him as he moved among friends. I watched him with his wife, I saw the love between them.

My Nephew, every once in a while the great game of politics moves from the issues of state that few can change – and most, like your father, care only to speak about, forsaking action for words. Just occasionally the game follows a different course, that of personal dilemma: the tragedy of a lost career, the destruction of a man's life and family. This was just such a moment, filled with farce and fear. The mob for an instant turned aside from their pleasures to tear a man apart, and the signal for them, my Nephew, came from his mistress.

She delivered her manifesto through the pages of a proper newspaper. She destroyed his career – not the one that was past, for in time he picked that up in much the same place as he had left off; no, she destroyed the career that he should have had.

Oh, Nephew, so much of politics is about what might have been. Why was this woman so vengeful? Who knows in truth whether it was the child, or words that he had spoken. Others have found themselves in her position and remained silent. No, I believe my friend had thwarted her own political ambitions, so that she failed to advance in a career in politics she believed could be hers.

Now, enough of all that. To return to the matter of Jermyn's Tea Rooms, I will tell you why I take you there, along with many others who I must say are of far greater import than you. There is a reason: the food is light and, I may say, ordinary; they serve no drink; and the chances of seeing any other politician there are slim, any journalist almost nil. And if indeed I did, by chance, find an example of either breed eating a ham salad and drinking a cup of coffee, they would believe whomever I entertained to be of no consequence whatsoever.

Your loving Uncle

PS How is your mother? By the way, your father spends rather too much time with his secretary. He dictates so many replies and receives so few letters that people are beginning to talk. I hear they dine at the Connaught, dance at Tramp's – people wonder where they sleep. She is far too young for him, and not nearly attractive enough to take such a risk for. Risk, I apologize, your father takes no risk. His career has been entirely composed of destroying the careers of others. He must be researching lust the better to spread vile rumours. And your sister, who does she sleep with these days? As for you, dear boy, is it boys or girls, or perhaps you still have not made up your mind? Perhaps you find me offensive. But bear this in mind, they will say far worse of you in the course of the career that you aspire to. Insider dealing, corrupt financial dealings, are you the hireling of a well-known crook, nominee chairman of some failing company, have you stolen from a pension fund, committed a fraud recently? They will say all of this about you. We will know that there is no truth in it, but still they will whisper, and as you grow older and prosper, marry and have children, soon the nameless ones (whom I could name) will attack you through your children. Still fancy a career in politics? Shall I continue to write to you, or will you set out for fame and fortune in a safer world? For in politics the risk is great, the gain is little. Although if, in truth, you are as I believe you to be, the gain for all of us will be immense.

There is a farm to be bought cheaply, not far from Oxford. I have always suspected that farming has its own rewards. Are you interested in the agent's address?

Your Uncle

Dear Nephew

I have heard nothing of you for the last few months – at least, nothing from your own hand. The columns of the *Daily Telegraph*, however, have kept me fully informed of how you spend your time at Oxford. Is it true that you dress in outlandish clothing, were so inebriated that you could not sit upright during a debate at the Union, let alone speak coherently? Am I to believe this? Do not offer to me the excuse that your colleagues on the committee were worse dressed and even more drunk than you. I have met one or two of them, and though I do not find that hard to believe, true or false, it is no excuse: your behaviour was, in my view, deplorable. I know that your father wrote and told you so, suggested indeed that the record of your behaviour would probably debar you from holding any worthwhile position in government. The old humbug, I have seen him worse drunk than you could possibly imagine, and, what is more, sober and worse behaved than you could ever possibly have been. Talent was the barrier that kept him from office – the lack of it. Talent will pave your way to office and principle will make your tenure of it worth remembering.

Do not feel that I am censorious in the matter of your behaviour. In my quiet sort of way I rather admire it. I wish that I had a head for drink; sleep, I am afraid, quickly removes me from the path of indiscretion. I do recall one night when, I may say, I was a deal older than you. I had visited my club, not in the evening but for lunch, and fell in with congenial company. Time passed, it was a Friday night, and by ten o'clock dinner was served, eaten and the club deserted except for me and my companion – or so we thought, until we came across a junior minister, a man of Greek extraction who has done well for himself and now passes as an Englishman with centuries of breeding. Do not think me a snob, only believe me when I tell you there is no greater snob than he. No matter. He was entertaining that night a quantity of the ladies from his constituency – a strange place to have so many women, a club that makes them enter by the back stairs, but it was his club and if he wished to entertain them there on a Friday night, who cares? No one.

My companion and I stood at the doorway of the dining room, listening to his peroration. The ladies applauded, he rose, bowed from the chest and quietened their applause. My companion applauded and the ladies applauded. Each time their applause eased, my companion and I encouraged its regeneration by applause of our own. We continued thus for ten minutes, the waves of applause came again and again, until the junior minister – realizing I suppose that he was receiving an ovation more suited in length to the speech of a man who led a great political party at its conference than to an after-dinner speech to women in a men's club – searched for the true cause of all this applause, spotted us and, guessing our part, in his embarrassment had us ejected. It mattered little, for I could not remember the occasion until my memory was refreshed along with my palate by the club's barman. This incident is, Nephew, an example of the humour of drink finding greater favour with the drunks themselves than with any other.

Fear not the consequences of your bad behaviour, just try to avoid those consequences by avoiding such behaviour. What is done is done, dear Nephew. But let there be something learnt out of this. Never read what the papers say of you. If they abuse you, take no notice. In short, when you reach high office do not read the newspapers, for their opinions are of no use to you, and as for news, you must make it, not wait for journalism. Waste not your time or your money on newspapers. Read the tapes for information, listen to the news, always be well informed – all of which is entirely different from knowing the opinions of writers.

My Nephew, you have not long now at Oxford, soon you must move on. Find gainful employment – gainful in the sense of what that employment can teach you. When you leave you need to have made only one decision, and that, what kind of man you will be. I have tried to set out for you the spectrum of human fallibility. The yes man, the political opportunist, both can do well for themselves. I cannot tell you how to conduct your life; you must choose. I can tell you that I believe you have it in you to be a man of principle, a prince among men. That sounds rather grand; it is in fact the reverse, for once you have chosen you are the slave of those principles. They will drive you, direct you, hurry your progress through life, and perhaps destroy you. They will narrow your range of choice in adversity, and if you dare to face dragging these principles like shackles with you, then indeed you may be a ruler of men.

Finally, my Nephew, take no notice of your father, but kiss your mother's forehead and smile. Your parents care how you behave, and I am bound to say that they care a great deal. You have hurt them. That cannot be helped, it is gone – but realize what you have done, for only when you admit a mistake to yourself can you set about remedying it. The older you get, the higher your office, the better the reasons for refusing to admit anything – thus the greater the necessity of admitting mistakes when you make them. Let the lesson of your indiscretion at Oxford teach you how to behave. Treat your electorate as you will now treat your parents. A nation's electorate and a man's parents have much in common.

Enough of that. Let me turn to your sister's inamorato, or little prig, whichever you may wish to term him. I suppose that he calls himself her fiancé – whatever, the little brute pesters me to get him on the candidates' list. I can think of nothing I am less likely to do. Even if I suffered from senile dementia, some internal reflex would make me work like the very devil to keep that awful man from trying his hand with the electorate. I don't suppose you could persuade him to join another party? I fully admit that many of our members in the House of Commons are quite as awful as he is. The fact is, dear Nephew, that I believe we should not have any more of them.

Your Uncle

PS My love to your mother, and under no circumstances tell her that I approve of your behaviour. I am supposed to be a serious man.

Dear Nephew

I was interested in your news from Oxford, your comings and goings, successes and apparent lack of failure, how well you have done, how well you appear to have done. There is no doubt that you are clever, you have proved that in the eyes of your contemporaries. You conduct your life in a manner close to brilliance, against them you compare very favourably. But remember this, Nephew, Oxford is a world unto itself, populated by those who know nothing and by those who know far too much. Take care, for a giant in that cloistered society can speedily turn into a pygmy when confronted with the hard words of politics.

You will not learn humility at Oxford, for it is not taught there. You have become the President of the Union, and I congratulate you. You intend to be prime minister, and I applaud your ambition, but I suspect that your knowledge of mathematics may be less developed than your facility with classical languages. Count the number of presidents that the Union has had, let us say since the First World War, and compare that number with the sum of its presidents who have become the prime minister of this country. Not very good odds, is it?

Nephew, I do not put down those who would be clever for I know full well, as this century draws to a close, that to lead this nation you need to have brains, and to have been taught in a formal sense how to use them. Guile and cunning – those attributes are largely God-given, although practice and observation will improve your ability to use them. I have told you before that all of these qualities go to make up a successful politician, but they are not the sum, for they lack the most important quality of all – principle. Without principle you very likely will not succeed, and if by chance you should, what would be the point of it? Where will you take this nation? Political life is not a race, an attempt to reach the end still in a position of power and influence. The aims of a political life should be to lead this nation on a well thought out route that will bring peace and prosperity to its citizens, ensure freedom under its laws, not least freedom from those who would impose their will on them. To lead a government which knows it has to respect the citizen, to respect a nation's history and institutions, to allow our citizens to feel respect for the nation, to bring glory to that nation. More important still, all of this should be conducted with honour.

I hear you laugh – what politician would give a handful of nuts for all that? I hear you say, we know of politics here at Oxford; that I am speaking of a world that does not exist. I speak of a world that should exist, of a world for which, if you have the ability (I believe that you have), the courage (who can tell if you have that) and the intellect (you can develop intellect), you can achieve all this. If you should fail, not by trying some cheap and convenient alternative, but fail for honest reasons, then your failure will be as great as any success. The course of principle is not an easy one. It involves taking actions that all will tell you are doomed to failure, for in the matter of principle there is no choice.

I enjoy your letters, Nephew. They are filled with gossip. I have spent my life enjoying gossip, placing sentences together like a jigsaw, each piece from a different source, none of them aware of what they contribute. Collected together, these twigs of gossip become a club to beat a rival, or, just for the fun of it, to swipe some politician who stands gawking at history as it passes him by.

I do not aspire to greatness. I have no ambition nurtured by success at the Oxford Union. The prime minister's job is not one that I covet or ever have coveted. When you write to me, write of your philosophies – but not pages and pages: if they are more than a line or two long, cast them aside, for what's on page one I will have forgotten by the end of page three. Short, simple, patently honest, that is how philosophy should come from the pen of one who would govern. Write to me in those terms or write not at all.

You are a golden youth, and in time you will learn the disadvantages of this. For the moment it seems to provide all that you need: a small fame, a multitude of friends who are also your admirers. Promotion comes your way because you stand out amongst your contemporaries. One day you will realize how you loved this praise, how you revelled in the applause of your peers, and you will be tempted to follow the course that brings that applause, that praise, that enthusiasm, and their love.

I was an ugly youth. At the time I suffered, or in my youthful foolishness I thought that to be the case. In time my ugliness became my asset. I understood rejection, I understood spite, I learned how to use both of these. Nephew, come to terms with loneliness. It will be a hard lesson for you, because you are companionable, you attract with your fine looks and sharp mind. In time you will have to take actions that will make your admirers into detractors, your friends into strangers, and those from whom you habitually seek praise your greatest critics. Your principles will demand that you take those actions that seem likely to cause you so much grief.

Nephew, practise now the art of loneliness. Remember always, when your eyes are closed as you search for sleep at night, that there is only one companion whom you sleep with, one friend, one admirer, one adviser, one judge, and those men are all one man, and that one man, my dear Nephew, is yourself.

How hot it is this spring – my plants wilt in the heat. I need to water the window boxes twice a day or my plants die in their wooden coffins hung four storeys up in the putrid city air. How London stinks of fumes from vehicles. I spent the weekend with your mother and nearly died of hay fever – she had brought the entire garden into her house. I argued with your father, or rather with the contents of his whisky bottle. I do believe that man has not a thought in his head that does not come straight out of a bottle of the Macallan's. By Sunday your mother was in tears.

I must say that I agree with your father about one thing, that wimp your sister drags around with her, ugly little brute. How many inches tall is he? I imagine that he is not technically a dwarf but close to it, damn close to it. That man is as opinionated as hell – where on earth did she find such a minuscule monster? Well, you can imagine he upset your father and myself. She, your sister, repeated some pretty awful home truths to your mother. Well, then we had the tears, your mother cried, your sister cried. I suggested, to be helpful you must understand, that if all this wailing did not cease then the midget was in danger of drowning in their tears. They all walked out, mother, daughter and that well-fed little prig. Your father was not walking anywhere, he could not stand let alone walk. He stayed and drank, I stayed and talked, heigh-ho, happy families.

So here I am back in London, in an airless room in an airless flat, in an airless city observing a government that would tear itself to bits if it had the courage. A government that believes a 'principle' to be the headmaster of a school. There are moments when I wish that they were unprincipled, but I am afraid they have not the wit for that. They just amble about dealing with this or that as it comes to mind, treating success as their own, failure as if it did not happen but were some lie that others tell about them. They are snide and seedy, all the while pretending niceness. Worse still, they are unutterably boring.

How on earth did you come to find that young man for your sister? Do not protest that he found her or she him, for they both separately and with some delight told me that you made the introduction. Do you have a secret talent for black humour? Be awfully careful of humour, black or white, it is a most dangerous commodity.

Your Uncle

Dear Nephew,

I write this to you on your father's death – out of sympathy for you on the loss of a father. As you know, I had no respect for the man and have not now that he is dead. He was your father, you will feel differently.

Nephew, the death of your father means that now you begin to be your own man. You may not realize it, but your life has changed. In time your mother will die as well. At that time all links with your past will be severed. There is left only you and your future.

With deep love,
Your Uncle

Dear Nephew,

It is now one year since your father died. I have received no reply to my letter of condolence. I regard this as bad-mannered at the best, a calculated rebuke at its worst. I trust that the absence of a communication from you is intended to be the latter, not just a slip of memory.

I have always admired you for your aggressive defence of your principles – it is a quality in you which I have tried to encourage. I was wrong to speak as I have of your late father. Wrong by the standard of convention, right by the standards that I have set myself. My criticism of him was no off the cuff judgement, nor indeed was it based on the fact that I never liked him. When I wrote to you I had reviewed the case both for your father and against him, I considered the words that I used, and still I wrote them down. This letter may seem to you written as an apology; it is not. An explanation, certainly, an apology, never, nor, dear Nephew, do I expect an apology from you. In another man I would let the whole matter fade amongst the diversions of a summer spent in Northern Italy, and on my return to London never think of it again, but with you, dear Nephew, it is different. Your mother keeps asking me if I have written to you. I find no difficulty in dealing with that question, but, not satisfied, the dear woman asks, have I received a missive from you. I find this hard to answer without causing her distress.

There is in life little as tiresome as he who would try to repair a breach in friendship between two men before their quarrel has run its course. Anger at a friend must burn like a fever – perhaps the friendship dies or, with time, in the way that fevers do, the anger burns itself out. The weakened friendship builds again, but surgery is never a good way to cure such ailments. That which is artificially put together will always remain artificial.

Your mother, poor dear, is desperate that no rift should appear in our relationship. She worries about your career and believes that I have a part to play in the making of it. She is concerned about my ageing and who will help me in infirmity. To you, dear boy, she has allocated that role. No doubt these propositions do little to please you. However, I have a suggestion. Why do we not dine at my club Thursday next? The food is passable and I have some bottles stored there, bottles of sufficient quality to win the friendship of an editor or two, sufficient even to drag more words than he intends from a colleague. No, do not refuse me – we might be able to reconcile our views without either of us moving far from our ground; alternatively, and this is an old and well used rule of life, you must spoil the Egyptians, eat their food, till their land and reap their crops: drink my wine, listen to my words, there may be something to be learned from them. Eight o'clock in the bar. Be prompt for they do not like you to dine at the centre table after eight-thirty p.m.

Dear boy, I have spoken of your mother. I admit it, she is but a camouflage. I have always loved you. I miss you, I miss your letters, yet under no circumstances allow the word love to influence your attitude to me – follow my words not out of love, but out of respect.

Your Uncle

Dear Nephew,

How long and hot this summer is. The days start before the dawn and end long after the sun has set. I wander in Italy, eat in a dozen *trattorie*, take the cool air of her churches and marvel at paintings I have seen a thousand times. I was the first into Lucca this year, just a day or two ahead of that motley crew, the British politicians and those who hang around them. First they came in a trickle, then a flood; they come to see each other, and when they return to Westminster they are filled with the glories of Europe, a continent which they extol endlessly, much to the irritation of those who have travelled further than just across the 'English' channel to take a holiday.

To add insult to injury, they call those who, by chance or intention, have travelled to many lands 'little Englanders'. Those wretched summer migrants to Tuscany who sit cooling their hands clasped around a glass of Pimms, beside a lemon tree, passing comments on the glory of Italy – what do they know of Italy's suffering, of the cancer that grips Italy's soul?

How I resent the necessity of my return to the office, how I resent this morning's visitor. He dropped his poison pill, barely greeting me before announcing that the manager of the hotel in Lucca had questioned him as to my whereabouts. He could not help, he said; he would not have helped, I thought. An urgent message from my office awaits me in Lucca – an unpaid bill, some mail marked confidential, it was about one or other of those matters. Which one? I asked. I would have pretended that I did not care, but I care desperately, I am too inquisitive to let a matter like this pass with style. He was not sure. I pressed him, he gave another list of headings that the manager's enquiry might come under. He told me nothing, but that nothing has destroyed my peace of mind. I contacted that hotel's manager and he recalled someone asking after me, someone who left no message, but who sounded vexed not to reach me. I must ring and find out about this matter, but for heaven's sake who shall I ring? I could make a spectacular fool of myself ringing my masters to enquire, did they have need of me in August? No, they would say, one after the other, what gave you that idea? Nothing of importance happens in August. To the devil with them all – nothing of any consequence except in the matter of assassination and declaration of war. Well, it cannot be that important, surely I would hear of such an event even in Italy?

My Nephew, when you become embroiled in this business of politics you will know just how I feel, for the true politician needs to know when an event will take place, where it will take place, and to be informed immediately that that event has taken place. News to the true politician is an addiction quite as compelling as the worst of drugs, quite as damaging to the health. Where there was peace in my soul, now there is turmoil, and when I speak of news I am not, my Nephew, referring to matters of great moment, for our lives are made easy, or some would say uneasy, by the constant flow of news from the great nations of the world. When we turn on the tired television set that sits each day in each room of even cheap hotels, out comes a flood of news.

No, Nephew, the news we need is the news leaked from Cabinet rooms, broadcast from country-house weekends, whispered at cocktail parties, pronounced by the truly ignorant as, bored with discussing wine and the killing of animals, they sit and tell each other how it goes in politics.

Some backbencher, who is no closer to the confidence of the Prime Minister than the editor of *Exchange and Mart*, enlightens those who listen to his words as if he were party to every thrust of government strategy. The tragedy of the whole sad affair is that, in his ignorance, the man is likely to be right. One thing is sure: the Prime Minister does not know what he is about to do this time tomorrow, let alone what his strategy is for the coming autumn. Should he hear of this ignorant backbencher's views, and they seem to be well spoken of, he will likely adopt them as his strategy, blaming the media for leaking them. Every disaster he claims as a triumph, for the reason that it forces a change of policy, and if that new policy has about it the slightest sign of success, the wretched leader of our Party, the Prime Minister of Britain, claims that the whole matter was a well laid plan. In order to stay ahead in this uncertain game it is quite as important to hear of the follies that are spoken as it is to hear the words of wisdom.

I shall arrive in Venice as this letter reaches you. Check my flat for mail, speak to my secretary or the girl who stands in for her if she has not returned from holiday. Any messages, notes, even the hint of communication, send it on to me at the Accademia hotel.

How is your dear mother? I will write to her under separate cover. And your foolish elder sister? The young and pretty one I saw at the airport as I left England. She headed for Greece with a band of young people. Lear would have found them useful models for his Albanian Brigands. I have seldom seen such a bunch. I fear for her in that company. When does she return? Where on earth did she find friends that seem so unsuitable? I have no date for my travels' end, but when I have I will pass it to you and we will dine in London; my club will have reopened by then.

Your Uncle

Dear Nephew,

I am very worried about your younger sister. There has been no word of her for some time. Your mother puts me off. She tells me that all is well, but frankly I do not believe her. I want no reassurance, I need facts. Where is she? Who is she with? Is she well? When did you last hear of her? When did you speak to her? I am worried, and shall remain so until I have solid evidence of her well-being.

Your mother speaks of no one but your elder sister and of nothing more than the excitement of her wedding to that appalling dwarf. He, incidentally, rings my office to invite me to lunch. He, it seems, needs to talk to me in lieu of your father, pathetic creature. How on earth could I sit trapped at a table and listen to his sanctimonious opinions? He says that he wants nothing and has no interest in the money that your sister inherited, or indeed the rather larger sum that will come her way on the death of your mother, yet he needs to know the details of it, the exact details. He does not like to raise this subject with anyone other than myself. He tries to placate me by the suggestion that I am discreet, that I understand how men think.

Discreet I have never been, careful only not to tell what I have no knowledge of; as, working in this place, those who chatter believe that I have knowledge of all things, they believe my silence to be discretion. He believes I understand how men think. I understand only too well how that tacky little ferret thinks; as for other men, most that I have met think not at all, and when they do the result is disaster. As for advice to your future brother-in-law, I could advise him, and if I did it would be not to relax in his sexual activity. Your sister clearly enjoys it.

My advice to your sister is, enjoy herself: if this minuscule creature gives her pleasure, enjoy that pleasure, and in time, when his ability wanes and her pleasure palls, having no contract, throw the wretched little fellow on the scrap heap of life. Your sister, I am afraid, is destined for a series of such adventures; it would be a shame if she lost her wealth at the first encounter.

Once, Nephew, in a letter to you, I wrote of politics, that you receive what people believe that you should receive, rather than that which you desire. That adage appears also to be true of life. However, I suspect that there is too much justice in that proposition. Neither politics nor life are that simple. In politics, success is invariably judged by other people's standards. The ordinary practitioner of politics would consider this success. True success is the carrying out of your aim with no compromise; to rise in politics it is necessary to dance with many partners, but as you dance they must embrace your objective, and you, my Nephew, if you cannot find partners to dance on your terms, you must sit by the wall and dance not – that is success.

Dear Nephew, life being as it is, your aim being pure, life is close to putrid. You may, of course, adjust your steps to dance conveniently with a partner. There is no need to damage a toe, provided the dance goes in the right direction, but remember this: compromise is a seductive creature clad in the paint and garments of congratulation, the praise of enemies. Principle wears tatters torn by the tongues of those who fear that principle will show them for what they are – children of the easy way.

Your Uncle

PS Please send news of my beloved niece, your younger and most wonderful of sisters.

Dear Nephew,

I can only say that I greeted with sadness the letter your mother sent in joy. Am I perverse? I do not believe so. I hate the little man – why? I have no reasonable answer to that question. Perhaps the question provides its own answer: I hate the fact that I even think about him. Hate myself for thinking about him, and so hating him is the unavoidable consequence of his intrusion into my life. Prepare yourself, dear Nephew, for your sister's next great adventure along the woodland path of her life.

You, my Nephew, walk a stony road and walk it carefully. For as you step upon each stone, remember that the stones you tread on as a youth may well be turned up and slung at you as you stand at the threshold of success. Walk carefully, my Nephew, leave deep footprints so that all can see where you have trod, leave no loose stones available to those who would stop you from your purpose. Far better to become a farmer now if you wish idly to kick stones as you walk through life.

Nephew, I write of serious matters, not whether or not your sister marries some fellow who appears to be an adventurer. I write to you of how you must construct your life, your political life, for setting on that course you have no other. You are on course to become the master of events not, as the present prime minister is, a mendicant to them.

No, Nephew, when you have your idea, events must become its servants. It is of that idea that I write. Have you considered a government of principle? You will ask, what is new in that, all governments set out to be principled? Do they succeed? Of course not, how could you expect them to, it is the task of politicians to twist and turn, to compromise and so to achieve; any other course would be folly. Is that what you believe? I do not blame you, Nephew, most others take that view. I myself have often enough had to follow that path, but it is not the way for you.

Compromise is seen these days as a great virtue; those who refuse to compromise are at the best tiresome men who prolong discussion, waste time that could otherwise be enjoyed in using the fruits of compromise, or, at worst, they are individuals consumed by bitterness seeking revenge for imagined wrongs.

Do not, Nephew, dismiss this analysis, for men of principle are rare and they have their fellow travellers just as the trimmers and compromisers have theirs. Men of principle are born such, but even so principle will not flourish without training and encouragement.

Take honesty, for example. A man is honest or dishonest, he cannot be a degree or two either way. Honesty, I am afraid, is the same as pregnancy; you, my Nephew, are either honest or dishonest, your sister is either pregnant or not pregnant. Once the action is taken there is no choice in the matter, your state becomes a fact of your life.

Take the man who will, I hope, be thrown from office. There is not a view in the spectrum of politics that he does not appear to agree with. You cannot charge him with intellectual dishonesty for he has no intellect. You cannot charge him with plain dishonesty because the fellow has no concept of honesty. Honesty, Nephew, is a commodity not much found in politics or among politicians. Your mother, God bless her, often a stupid woman taken by frivolous and tiresome notions, understands honesty. All your life, you may have bemoaned her creed, but it is inherent in your upbringing, you understand honesty; to be dishonest needs for you a conscious action.

I have good news. You are accepted for the list of candidates for our Party. Please send £32 soonest.

You will now set out on the troop around the constituencies who see candidates for the next election. The political research centre will take a relaxed view of your absence from work in search of a seat. This job will help you as you seek election to Parliament, but will be of little use once you sit there. You have come to politics too soon in life, you know I disapprove. But then, politics has become a profession where once it was a vocation. We will likely lose, and in any case it would be unusual for your first constituency to be winnable, so it will be some years before you join the national Parliament. Nephew, that is to your advantage. Many will announce their retirement in the next couple of months, stick their votes in the back of their leader as he stands for re-election by his Parliamentary Party, then they will head for a bundle of directorships. Seats in plenty will be vacant after the next election, so approach their selection committees with directness. Do not try to please today, for today's pleasure will be displeasure tomorrow. Tell those people what you believe in, talk of your beliefs as you believe in them, no easy answers, no avoiding issues – risk rejection. Tell them your truth and then give them hope, for hope is the point of government, hope is the reason for power. Without hope, why would anyone elect you, and if no one will elect you, why on earth should these people select you? In time we will work out exactly how that hope is to be defined; at this time, suffice to say that it will not be delivered by deception. There will be no conjuring tricks, no words with false bottoms or the other paraphernalia of the trickster, no double meaning, no sleight of hand. When you stand and speak, tell them that what they hear is what you will deliver or resign, for yours is the politics of principle, and in time yours will be a government whose policies will have a moral basis. I hear my colleagues laugh. I wonder whether they will laugh as they tramp the streets of the City of London in search of former friends to beg for employment. The end draws near for the charlatans in our party.

Nephew, I am desperate for news of the younger of your sisters. Your mother puts me off with sensible words. I am sure that all is not well with her – have you no knowledge of where she hides?

Your Uncle

Dear Nephew

I enjoyed travelling to Blackpool with you. Your company made that tedious journey by railway easier to bear, your conversation was as always entertaining.

Nephew, be careful of jokes; humour does not help a career. Under no circumstances pass your *bon mot* about the PM to any other. As soon as I have written these few words I will cast it from my memory. It has, I am afraid, real quality, the sort of slight that, even delivered by one of such little consequence as yourself, could severely damage him. I laughed for several days; if that joke gained currency the man would have little alternative but to hide his head for weeks. A joke like that could finish a career, and your career, dear Nephew, is far too fragile for you to allow yourself to play any part in the destroying of a career as old as the PM's.

Nephew, what a conference. What a tangle of plot and counter-plot – there can hardly have been a minister in the hall on Friday who did not have his own agenda. Yes, they all gave the PM a rousing ovation, held up flags, cheered him to the rooftops for just the right amount of time with just the right amount of volume. Music is the secret of these events, the holiday tunes as the audience waits, the patriotic airs as the PM enters, his speech, and then the music turns to the triumphant strain, the audience chants and claps in time, the PM makes his progress through the crowds. I have seen the eyes of that man's greatest enemies fill with tears. What a speech he made, turgid rubbish from start to finish. He would have been better employed reading out a telephone directory – that at least would be suited to his style. Take no notice of the final applause; watch and listen during one of these speeches, see how the audience reacts to the man, not the production. I have seen a PM make a speech ten times the quality of that speech and be forced from office. The electorate who sit in that hall are not the electorate who make and break prime ministers. The fate of party leaders hangs on the votes of their party in the House of Commons; to assume otherwise is folly. True, the members of Parliament consult with their constituency chairmen and other party officials. However, they interpret these consultations in the light of their own careers. The prejudices of a parliamentary party decide who leads them. The secret consultations are private to the members themselves and they will report opinion in their constituency in a way that supports their own opinions.

Each year in office a prime minister accumulates enemies – a sacking here, a slight there, someone being passed over for promotion. Usually matters of self-interest motivate these people. Oh, they dress it up, consult, ask advice, and then do as they secretly wish. It's a shameful business, unseating a prime minister, but these men and women weigh carefully the political odds, assess their own advantage and then go about that shameful business with gusto.

No, that man may have seemed secure to you, and to most others, last week, but I tell you that he will be gone before November is out. His going will not be easy, for the only certainty in his whole existence is the knowledge that he wishes to hold on to office. There has been no compromise that he has not made or will not make to hold on to it. He rather grandly calls these compromises negotiations. He has governed as a coalition, with odds and ends from other parties helping his legislation on to the statute book. On more than one occasion he has co-opted the Opposition to his cause. He lacks conviction, he lacks principle, and his policies lack a moral basis, but the man has cunning in profusion, he most certainly does not lack cunning.

I know how it will go. He will talk of his achievements, even his failures he presents as achievements. Changes of policy forced on him become examples of his wisdom, his desire to balance, to compromise. He will promote the idea of how much worse the past would have been without his steady hand. How any alternative leader of our party would be further to the right wing (he says this to frighten the left) or more to the left wing (he says this to frighten the right). His opponents find him hard to fight because they do not know where he stands. He has words that appeal to every shade of political colour – words: like Jimmy Durante, the man has a million of them. Then, atop all this confusion, he claims to be a winner. He has won nothing except the votes to keep himself in office, and implicit in this is the fact that the members of his parliamentary party who vote for him will keep their seats; if he goes, they go, or so he tells them.

So, I suppose life being what it is, the man may stay. Throw him out on his ear, say I, let us set about repairing the damage of his years in office.

Nephew, it was well that we spoke about the younger of your sisters. I did not know of the rift in your family, and I am sad that she no longer speaks to your mother. They are both making the most awful mistake. I understand how your mother feels – a man twice your sister's age with no employment is a hard pill to swallow, but swallow it she must if your sister is to be saved from unhappiness. The man, it seems, is given to violence. I cannot understand your sister's attitude in support of him when he threatened your mother. What you tell me of the accommodation that they occupy and the district where they live fills me with horror. Your sister was always so meticulous in her cleanliness. What hold does this man have over her? Does he beat her? It seems from your description of her face that he does. You must think carefully how to deal with this matter. It seems to me too dangerous a situation to be allowed to run its course in the hope that her love will fade. Keep me informed, but under no circumstances tell your sister that I know these things. In time she may wish to change the style of her life, and I wish to cause her as little

[41]

embarrassment as possible when that happens. May God keep her safely in the meantime, for I fear her future is in his hands. I pray for her and your mother.

Dear Nephew, I listened with care to your conference speech. You chose the subject well. Law and order is a winner with selection committees the country over. Good rough and tumble stuff you gave them, plenty of drama, gestures at the right moments. A well timed speech for a beginner. But something was missing. Do you know what that something was? I doubt it, for the speech had no thought in it, it was totally lacking in intellect, in idea. As a result it passed unreported, and an unreported speech is a wasted speech. You have attended a party conference, spoken, been well received, yet your career has not improved by one jot or one tittle. You have passed up a great opportunity.

Now, Nephew, this is what you must do: take your speech and tear it up. Start again, examine the moral basis for a policy on law and order, proceed to a conclusion as to how that problem should be handled, put that in with a few of the remarks from your first effort. A small quantity of histrionics never goes amiss, nor do they ever distract attention from the words that are the message. Never swamp your speech with rhetoric – leave your audience with ideas that they can remember, not just with a feeling of good will. There is no harm in repetition – repeat, repeat, repeat and repeat that speech everywhere you go, this year, next year. For each new speech take the moral basis of your subject and the conclusions that flow from that. So will you make speeches, so will you make your career.

God bless you, my Nephew. I am sorry that we could not travel home together. The PM asked me to fly with him in a plane that some nobility had lent him. I must say, the fellow may well be stinking rich, but the champagne he left on board for us was extremely ordinary. The PM called for a second bottle – happily we landed before the pilot could find one. We must dine next week at the Travellers.

Your Uncle

Dear Nephew

I wish you luck at the selection committee meeting next week. I have little advice for you as to how you should present yourself, only that if you take exactly the opposite line from the sitting member that usually pleases them.

You cannot dissemble, however. Remember that your constituency and your majority will become your power base. Far better you show them who you really are. Once, a complete crook acquired a safe seat in the simplest way. The constituency had by mistake selected a member of an extremist group; embarrassed by this, they quickly deselected him. So began the process of his replacement, and, anxious not to make the same mistake again, they consulted my office. Well, as you can imagine we had just the man, a real deadbeat, who fitted every criterion that the Party would like to apply to members of its Parliamentary Party. So all was arranged, the gentleman proposed by the office appeared before the committee and made a long, rambling but acceptable speech – just acceptable. He praised the government, its policies and its members, he praised the Party, and he indicated that he would be prepared to offer allegiance to whomever or whatever his constituency party might require, and he took his time about all this.

Next came a woman, rather an attractive woman, a dummy put in by the Party. Selection committees are largely made up of women, and by and large they do not select other women, especially attractive ones.

The third candidate was inarticulate, right-wing and did not make a good impression at all; he was chosen by the office for just these attributes.

The area agent sat watching the proceedings, giving just a nod here or a cough there. This man felt sure that the candidate he had responsibility for would be selected by a robust majority. He would have been, for he appeared by far the best of the three and that was not saying much. The constituency chairman who chaired the selection committee listened to the last of the candidates speak. The chairman came to the same conclusion as the area agent, I suppose hoping to win fame at Party Headquarters, then, to his great surprise, to find himself rewarded by having the letters CBE affixed to his name.

The chairman asked the inarticulate candidate a question. 'What do you see as your course of action if we select you as our candidate?' Then, so I am told, he leaned back in his seat with a look of satisfaction. All present expected a long, rambling answer; in return they received one short sentence. 'I see as my duty to carry out the work of God in Parliament and there to represent the interests of my constituents.' The man was selected. He turned out to be the most awful crook, but never mind, that was not the purpose of my story. Rather to explain to you that the two qualities the electorate admire most are purpose and principle.

Tell those people of your principle and your strength of purpose. Tell them that there has to be a moral aspect to all policy. Do not speak of policies, do not speak of personalities, do not make promises, just show them how you will judge each issue, show them that your philosophy gives you no room for manoeuvre, but equally show them that, because you have a philosophy, you do not have to consider how you will react as each issue arises.

Good luck, my Nephew. Worry not if you meet rejection – far better that you learn about rejection now, far better that you accept rejection rather than engage in a humiliating search for praise.

I am worried, dear boy, about your younger sister. How often have I written these words? Perhaps I am old, living in a different age, she must know that what she does is wrong, or why would she not tell me of it? I followed her from the hovel where she sleeps with that terrible fellow. I disguised myself. She may have known that she was followed but will not have guessed it was by me. I borrowed a raincoat of the office nightwatchman, a dirty fellow with clothes to match. She left her doorway at near enough eight-thirty p.m. She took the tube to Charing Cross Road, then on foot to Greek Street, where she disappeared into a building. I joined a group of men dressed much as I was. We watched the women who stood at the doorway by which your sister had entered. In thirty minutes your sister came out to join them and she wore a dress that floated above her knees. As she moved I saw suspenders and the dark tops of her stockings against the white flesh of thighs. She had been there but a moment when one of the group I stood with went across to speak to her. They turned and walked together back into the building. I take it to be a club. His arm was tight around her velvet bodice. I waited two hours. The weather was not cold, the wait far from boring.

Dear boy, I am not naive, I know these clubs. Lord knows I have often enough bought champagne at four times its price only to have the girl I sat with turn the half-empty bottle upside down in the ice bucket as she called for more. She will come to no real harm working there. I am sure that is what she believes. As for me, I know this is only a beginning, that she may sink or rise. She left the club with a man on her way to a nearby 'hotel'. There he was to give her a sum of money, she to promise him hours of pleasure; after their coupling of a few minutes she would pull on her dress and ask for a taxi fare home.

My Nephew, I am deeply affected to see my niece do what I have so often done. I felt revulsion at her behaviour that was only a mirror-image of my own. What I had once thought of as fun, as pleasure, now seems empty and terribly sordid. For lust is but conceit under another name. Lust is not and cannot be love. Pleasure from lust is a perverted pleasure. Pleasure from love is a pleasure without a price, a pleasure that can only be given.

I learned more that night, my Nephew, than the whereabouts of my niece. The man she went with, well, he seemed a better sort of man than the man she went home to. I deeply hope that the child knows what she is doing, and I pray that she takes care. Your mother must never know of this, nor, for that matter must your elder sister. She is insisting on lunching with me to show off her pale admirer. Truly, what kind of man is he? Not one I would willingly lunch with, of that I am sure.

By the way, the PM believes that his speech at Blackpool was a triumph. He told us all so, and those men and women of convenience who give him words to say smiled and started to think of more meaningless phrases for his next great offering to the Party and the nation

Your Uncle

Dear Nephew

I enjoyed dining with you last week. I must, however, in all
honesty, say that while you are an energetic and entertaining
guest, you certainly put yourself out in an effort to amuse.

There is the matter of how you dress. Mine is a liberal-
minded club, tolerant of affectation, indeed tolerant of
drunkenness and all the behaviour that flows from excessive
drinking. They do, however, like you to wear a tie. No, this is
no criticism of you, just that the members of the place seem to
have a thing about ties. You remarked as we dined, with some
justice, upon the vile colour of the club's tie; however, there
was no need to extend that criticism to those who wear such
ties. All of this you could have been forgiven – many present
would, on past form, have little recall of you or your jibes the
following morning. No, dear Nephew, it was your own tie
that caused the offence. It was, if I may say so, a creation
better fitted to fulfil the function of a bootlace. Some who saw
it round your neck believed it to be just that, probably helped
to that conclusion by the fact that there were no laces to keep
your boots on your feet. When you dine with me at my club I
expect a certain standard of behaviour. They are a good,
patient membership at the club, but you sorely tried that
patience.

Now, whether I approve or not of your looking like a
plumber taking a break for a meal halfway through repairing
the septic arrangements for a housing estate is a matter of no
consequence. What does matter is that you learn, and learn
quickly, that how you look is of vital importance. How you
look will help or hinder your ability to have your views taken
seriously. Wearing the outfit that you effected that evening
for dinner, you could perhaps have moved the political views
of a group of plumbers, but not those of a gathering of broad-

casters and the like. Judges and journalists have become, by the practice of their calling, cynical individuals: they see so much fraud, they observe the consequences of dishonesty, they can spot it for what it is. Do not try to disguise an education at Eton and Oxford with the clothes of a plumber. Wear the clothes men expect you to wear while thinking the thoughts that men do not expect of you. When you have power it is your action that will need disguising, not your character that must always be predictable. You will, dear Nephew, if you dress as those you meet at party gatherings, be selected by them as their candidate at the next election. Then you must win the voters' hearts. Dress as they expect you to dress and they will put you in Parliament – so will begin your real career.

Dear Nephew, when you sleep at night you are alone with the record of your thoughts. Have no conflict with them if you wish to rest. A rule for peaceful rest at night as good as any other is: never engage in mathematics after sunset, never engage your mind on a problem then try to sleep, for neither the solution that you find nor your night's rest will be truly satisfactory. Nephew, I have served long in this party's headquarters. I can tell you of many a trick to turn the tide in your favour. There must, however, be a point to this tide turning, there must be an idea that you wish to implement.

The path that we will plan together is a path that will lead you to become a true leader. Together we will risk all – settling for nothing less.

Your Uncle

Dear Nephew

Congratulations, you have achieved your first goal. God willing, and yourself showing a modicum of intelligence, you will, whatever the outcome of the next election, sit in Parliament.

I believe that election will be rather sooner than you imagine. My money is on the second week in May. Good weather and a new leader might even see us back in office. I dined last night with the chairman of the Twenty-two. He wished to mark my card. There is a challenge – not one, I think, that can succeed. However, once a challenge is made there is no knowing what, or rather who, will come out of the woodwork.

Dear boy, spend many hours with your constituency. Nurse it well, for come win or lose you must be sure to go to the Commons.

I have for the last two weeks followed your younger sister. She goes about her work, turning up each night at the same time, taking only one man to a hotel each night. She seems popular amongst those who patronize that club, and looks healthy. I am concerned only that the man she lives with beats her. Last night her crochet shawl fell from her shoulders and I noticed dark marks on her upper arms, a bruise on her face well camouflaged with paint. I followed her home on the late tube. Nephew, we must meet and plan how to deal with this matter. I know that you take a relaxed view of the whole affair. A modern attitude, an attitude I must tell you that is just not good enough. Not good enough at all. I know that you accuse me of interfering in her affairs. I resent the suggestion that I get some voyeuristic pleasure out of following her. You did not say it, rather you inferred that I get sexual pleasure by proxy. I reject this utterly. You, she, even I, we all need help, and I will tell you that as you grow older the number of those willing to offer it grows smaller by the hour.

I understand that you are full of yourself at the moment. You, however, cannot just opt out of your sister's life taking no responsibility for her welfare, that is not a moral attitude. I accept that interfering in the lives of others is objectionable to you. Interfering in the lives of others is objectionable to me. Here we have a problem; this girl we believe needs help because she does not conduct her life as we believe she should, which incidentally is not usually how we conduct ours. Should we leave her alone, taking the chance that her circumstances will deteriorate, that her life will move outside of her control, or should we act to force her to change her ways?

Reflect well on this problem that you have with your own family, for it is in microcosm a problem that you will encounter in the lives of others, of nations and of continents. In a nutshell, to what extent can people be trusted with their own lives? To what extent can nations be trusted to conduct their own affairs? To what extent can either nations or people be allowed to harm themselves or their own citizens provided that they do not harm their neighbours or, in the case of nations, other nations?

Your mother has written to me suggesting that we all spend Christmas together as a family. This, perhaps, will put a time limit on your deliberations. Remember, if you cannot decide the morality of your dealings with your family, how on earth will you ever decide the morality of our nation's dealings? You will, I am afraid, become just another politician, a slave of convenience.

I lunched two days ago with your elder sister. We ate at Simpson's in the Strand: good service, good food, wonderful wine (for the price), but the company was appalling. You well know that I find your sister tedious, that I have complete contempt for her fiancé, a man who sorely tries my patience.

[51]

Well, she excelled herself this time, bringing along a new friend and current protégé. I suppose you know him (if that is the case, I censure you for not tipping me off) – the longest, blackest Ghanaian that you have ever seen in your life. Well, certainly the largest I have ever seen. She thought to test me, to embarrass me, to demonstrate her liberal principles. The fact that the man was black meant nothing to me, it was his conceit that I could not stand. He knew about everything, informed on every subject with the best of English accents. He spoke what was once called BBC English, in the days before regional accents became fashionable. How I hated that man.

'He is a prince you know,' the wretched girl informed me. 'Who is?' I replied. 'He,' she said. 'My friend is from a princely family.' All of this in front of him. I misread the child. I thought that she intended to demonstrate the difference between her liberal youth and my prejudicial age. Not a bit of it. Your elder sister is just an old-fashioned snob. Then her friend tried to sell me life insurance, for that is what he is, a life-insurance salesman. Am I an old-fashioned snob as well, for detesting those who sell life insurance under false colours? In fact I do not care for them even when they sail under their own flag. 'This is not why we are having lunch,' say I. Our conversation wandered around aimlessly until that silly girl turned it to politics. 'Will the Prime Minister survive?' she asked, and without a moment's hesitation came her friend John's reply: 'Without a doubt.' The one your sister thinks to marry. She wants to marry everyone, or anyone, and to make them acceptable she does not think about them at all.

The PM has just rung me, he hears that there is to be a leadership challenge. Do I by chance know whom his opponents have chosen as their candidate? Could it by chance be the Chairman of the Party? I doubt it, I reply, but why not ask him to propose you, I suggest, that will smoke him out. The PM likes that idea. He will get the Foreign Secretary to second him. Well, there are two votes this pathetic man can be sure of. I must say, the man knows how to plot. I cannot conceive of him staying in power, but the Party are now about to engage in the only activity at which the PM excels.

Your Uncle

Dear Nephew

The wretched man won. Whoever would have believed it possible? Your sister rang me within minutes of the announcement just to point out that events have turned out exactly as her 'friend John' predicted. She wished to talk to me about investments that 'John' wishes her to make. Perhaps I could see my way to the trust funds being released. John, it seems, is of the view that I and the other trustees could have done better for her. That was what they really wanted to discuss at Simpson's, but it seems I insisted on talking about politics and the Ghanaian lingered too long at the table. Could we meet again? I told her that I am particularly busy till Christmas. Nephew, confirm that fact for me.

The Opposition will not move a censure motion this week. They will wait a week or two and then hit us with a debate on the social services. Cuts have to be made, and they know the Party is split on where those cuts should be. We could lose that vote, our majority is desperately thin as it is. The death last week of that junior minister was unexpected, and frankly there is no possibility of holding his seat. There is a disgruntled element in the Party who feel that we have been too long in power. Normally there are eight by-elections in a year; we have been lucky that this is the first of them so far. Lose this one, and if five others go we will become a minority government, left to die the death of a thousand bribes. There are men who would rather go honourably over an honourable issue than struggle on to an end that is inevitable, postponed only by months. The PM wastes his time telling them that the economy will be better in the spring: they regard his handling of it as a disaster. The right wish a government truly of the right and will happily swap this one that they believe to

[54]

be socialist for one that they know to be socialist. It will then be only a matter of how it is done.

Your Uncle

Dear Nephew

I have told your elder sister that I will not allow this man 'John' to organize her investments, even if they are engaged. The silly child cried and cried. I think that the time has come for you to explain that when I say no I mean no. I have not asked your mother to do this; you are the only man in the family and it is your duty. Do it with despatch. I have told her and I will tell you that I have the unqualified support of the other two trustees in this matter. She must come to terms with my decision or I shall have to speak to John myself. As it is, I have had to put up with a whole lot of rot about spoiling her life. There is only one element of this matter that is spoiled and that is your sister, thoroughly spoiled. I am quite sick and tired of her, and I have no more time to devote to this matter.

The PM has been causing me no end of trouble. He is full of self-conceit at winning the leadership ballot. The way he talks you would imagine that he had just seen off his bitterest rival, rather than a backbencher who has hardly been heard of before and certainly will never be heard of again. He does not realize the significance of what has happened. This backbencher of no account has shown the legitimacy of challenging a sitting prime minister. In our party, a prime minister will never be secure till the rules are changed to make that impossible. It can only harm us, this shooting at generals. The PM is now fair game for any political gunfighter who wishes to make a name by participating in his downfall. He, poor soul, imagines that the Parliamentary Party have just given him a vote of confidence.

The PM does not seem to realize that he won against a nonentity by the grace and favour of his rivals. The PM fails to see that these rivals can sink him whenever they choose; for the moment the PM is left to wither on the vine. He rants and

raves, practises speeches that he will never deliver and neg-
lects to practise those he must make in the coming weeks. The
wretched man will seize on a sentence, from a soap opera for
all I know, or written on the back of a menu taken from some
dinner given for cricketing cronies – 'This is what it is all
about,' he will pronounce. Then his staff, agreeing with him,
will take that banal offering and start rearranging its words.
At least Humpty Dumpty knew what he required of words in
the matter of their meaning. This man's staff seem not to care,
and he not to know. He calls all this his big idea – I am lost
for words, I fear he has too many friends who write poor
novels.

Nephew, you must take control of your elder sister, I
cannot have her about my ankles at this time. And Nephew, I
went again last night and watched my other niece. The one
that I truly love. Times are bad with her. She has left that club
where she worked. She is pale of face. She has lost much
weight. She has changed both her place of business and the
style of that business. I watched her talk to men in cars. Cars
that barely moved along the kerb of the road. I watched as
she sat beside them, as she and a man drove off together. I
waited for her return, sometimes in minutes, last night after
some hours. She seemed to have drunk alcohol – I hope that it
was alcohol that made her unsteady on her feet. I fear for that
child, Nephew. I have no notion of how to deal with this
situation.

I dined last week with the chairmen of two large companies. Dined very well I might say. They had only one question:
when will the PM resign? Make way for a winner – their
words, not mine. Nephew, we must prepare for Opposition,
for that man does not understand the nature of resignation.
He does not understand that there is a point beyond which
men of honour cannot go. He does not understand this
because he believes that men of honour are the production of
the fevered imagination of the likes of me. He once told me

[57]

so, told me quite clearly that every man has his price. He is right, of course, but he does not fully understand the matter. He does not realize that the price of honour is the reserve price put on a man's actions: the price below which he is his own man, the price beyond which he is yours.

This prime minister is a low bidder in a high-priced auction. He has, in fact, in this way created honour of a sort in what would otherwise be a dishonourable Cabinet. He understands the different currencies that the bids are made in, but he is destined to be an underbidder in life's auction. I would like to tell you that price is his problem. No, Nephew, conceit is the man's problem, conceit is his problem.

The captains of industry dine to the full. We drank a Latour 66 – it has lasted well, very well, in the large bottles. I can recall staying at the *châteaux* in that year. I saw those grapes as they hung on the vines, small, round, hard and bright green. What tremendous strength has the farm land that delivers a harvest which bottled becomes pure magic.

Nephew, always bear this in mind. The prettiest men are often the emptiest, the ugliest full of vigour and ideas.

Nephew, I seldom criticize your friendship, but I believe the group of young politicians you have taken up with are not the sort with whom you should spend your time.

Nephew, your mother tells me that we will all gather at Christmas. She suspects that something is up with your younger sister. This is the second time that she has mentioned Christmas. I assured her that I would be there, she assured me that all the family will be there. I am suspicious of her.

Your Uncle

Dear Nephew

The PM does not realize that a member of his Cabinet is about to resign. The man knows that we cannot win the election. He told me that he intends to arrange a few director-ships before the market is flooded with his colleagues. He asked for introductions, did I give him any? Of course I did. The PM knows little of Opposition. I and a few others are only too familiar with those barren years. By the time that you receive this letter we will once again be in a political crisis.

Your sister, the elder one, called me by telephone to suggest the nature of the Christmas present that I should give her. I watched again in the streets to observe how life goes with your younger sister – not well, I am afraid.

In haste.
Your Uncle

PS We will meet at Pratt's for dinner Thursday late ten-thirty, sausages, chips and claret.

Dear Nephew

You will have read all in the daily journals. The Secretary of State for Health and Social Security has set forth on a journey to more profitable employment. His replacement has been announced – all of this you will know. I can add to the newspaper reports, but not a word of this if you will to any other.

Well, the former Secretary of State's going was not an easy matter. The cunning man told the PM that he wished to resign his seat. You can imagine the trouble that caused, the comings and goings. The Party Chairman made it quite clear that circumstances do not exist under which we could hold that seat in a by-election, the PM offered him this and offered him that. The ex-Cabinet minister explained that it was not a question of houses or jobs, his was a resignation of principle. I know full well that it was not, the man told me so; however, I am unlikely to reveal that information. So now the man fully believes his own lies, and a matter of principle his resignation will be, unless ... The PM went through a whole list of 'unless'es until they came to the matter of a peerage. That will mean a by-election protested the PM. Not if I wait till the General Election to resign my seat. Ah, says the PM, the promise of a peerage. Yes, says his man, in writing, and so that is what he has been given, the promise of a peerage. Win or lose, written in the PM's own hand, signed at the bottom, dated at the top.

Nephew, you may have imagined that to be the end of the matter, not a bit of it. The real problem was finding a replacement. It is hard to believe, but there is little enthusiasm for that job these days. The woman who was appointed is not up to it, not because she is a woman, but because talent did not come into the debate, convenience was the criterion, availability, public impact as reported in the friendly Press, as recorded by the pollsters. This is the way things are done these days. This is the beginning of the end.

Nephew, I look forward to the Christmas recess. I cannot wait to get away from all of this. I will enjoy a fortnight debating with you, talking over what might have been, or even perhaps might be.

Love to your mother. I will arrive Christmas Eve on the four-thirty train, I expect you to meet me at the station. I will as usual bring with me one of the Bradenham black hams.

Your Uncle

Dear Nephew

Christmas did not go well. I know that all seemed to enjoy themselves, but I cannot stand false gaiety. In truth, your mother seems in a state of extreme depression. Her lies as to the whereabouts of your younger sister convinced no one; I suppose she knows more than she is letting on. Has there been any contact between them? Telephone calls? Letters? I must know all of the evidence in this matter, hold nothing back from me, tell me all.

As for your other sister. That girl has put on so much weight, she is becoming quite gross. Always a chubby child, then may I say a voluptuous young thing, she is speedily turning into a monster. As for her Ghanaian 'friend' – when that young man was not imposing his opinions on us, it was his feet that got in the way. Why, that young man, when he sits in an armchair, stretches halfway across the room. Why on earth did we have to share our Christmas with that man? I can understand friend John being there – he is, after all, the woman's fiancé; that was bad enough without her protégé being imposed on us.

I have to hand it to friend John, crude as his opinions are, they are close to the truth of the matter: the government will soon fall. The miners will not bring it down; this time it is to be the turn of teachers, nurses, even the police are not well disposed towards us. When a government of the right loses the support of the police, then that government had best consider carefully the actions that brought matters to that state.

The party of law and order must always be at one with those charged with maintaining law and order. However, our party has changed. There was a time when to be a member of our party meant to conserve the best of the past and to improve the rest. To radically look at the state of our nation with the idea of strengthening all that we hold dear – sound finances, sovereignty, free trade, law and order, and above all freedom under the law. Indeed, sometimes to risk our own freedom fighting for the freedom of others. Now principle has gone, morality is going, and who gets the blame? The very policies that made us strong, and we, Nephew, we wallow in our weakness, calling it compassion.

Talking of equality reminds one of such banal phrases as 'a nation at ease with itself'. What on earth does that mean? 'A classless society' – does such a thing exist? Could it be invented? No leaders, only followers following each other, or only leaders all going in different directions at exactly the same pace at exactly the same time – what madness is this? Is that what they, my masters, would give to us in place of philosophy, morality, direction? A government of opportunity, that is what we have, its members taking every opportunity to advantage themselves. They seize opportunity with both hands as it appears, tread on it with both feet, chase it with the speed of summer's lightning, with no thought as to the consequences of their actions. I wish that I could call them fools.

No, Nephew, these are not mindless men; they think long and hard in the matter of self-advancement. They deliberately neglect the inconvenient, the harder path. They have little interest in the success of our nation beyond the point where that success is useful to advance their own careers. Yes, Nephew, these men talk of social improvement, they have their own social agendas, because by nature they enjoy interfering in the lives and businesses of others. Even in their social aims they fail from lack of true conviction.

Why, you ask, are they members of our party, these parliamentarians who would interrupt a contract freely entered into between two willing parties? The answer is simply that these people are in our party only because they spotted that the nation's heart and mind was moving to the right of politics. These men and women who came to power on the back of the hot-blooded thought of the right – the policies of belief, of passion, of commitment – they are but fellow travellers who use the virtues of that politics to beat it about its own head. Slyly, they discredit that politics, telling the people that they have been misled, that there is an easier way.

These creatures who masquerade as our supporters are but thugs joining a party of travellers. During the day, making travelling pleasant, telling tales to entertain and pass the tiring journey, helpful in setting up the camp in the evening – and then at night murdering their new companions, stealing their goods, burying their bodies and setting out to deceive, rob and to squander on another day.

This, Nephew, is why I so hate those who would tritely trash our nation into what I see as a pit of despair. I tell you all this because I believe that your friends fall into the category of these politicians that I have written of – self-interested and self-seeking. You want my advice, Nephew: give up politics, go out and get yourself a job, learn about life and the people who wander through it, for you are about to shut yourself in a hothouse where men's heads are turned by the heat of their words. Those friends I spoke of, your friends, they know nothing, they have learned nothing. Hear them speak, they make this all clear. The truth is that if you are to succeed – and do not confuse that word with prosper – you must cut your own path, a moral path; every aspect of your policy must have a moral base. You do not need groups of eager young men and women to tell you right from wrong, that is a matter that is clear to you. As I have written to you before, right and wrong are not matters of degree. You either know the difference or you do not; too late, Nephew, to learn now, the difficulty lies in judging right and wrong.

Take the matter of your younger sister. Is her behaviour right or wrong? If you have no philosophy, no set of standards, how on earth can you tell? Clearly that girl is her own mistress, she can do with her body as she wishes. She broke the law only to a small degree, and broke a law that is not well enforced. Consider the problem; legally she is wrong, but by current values not terribly so. She has no religious conviction; Church of England by habit (a habit for some years discontinued), she has no traditional moral values of her own that she has broken – indeed, her personal moral values may allow her to follow this course of hers. Nephew, tell me the answer to this problem. I feel so sad for the girl. I had such hopes for her: she was to be a beauty, I loved her quick wit. Something must be done. But what, and, furthermore, by whom? She must be saved from herself. Nephew, it is your duty to address this matter.

The PM's Boxing Day lunch at Chequers was as usual all cricketers and bit players from the media. They came, I think, to look at the pictures. The PM enjoyed himself mightily. They all told him how wonderful he was, and I suppose on the way home told each other how appalling he is.

Many thanks for the books you gave me for Christmas. How on earth did you manage to find a copy of Alan Watkins's *A Conservative Coup*? It all seems so long ago. By the way, I left behind the soap that your elder sister gave me, could you bring it to London when you come? As for her new friend's gift, he drank it before I left. I am rather glad really, for what on earth would I do with it? I could not drink it myself, nor could I give such a dubious bottle to a friend, and my daily's husband, well trained on my cellar, has far too good a palate for that rubbish.

Your Uncle

Dear Nephew

I write to congratulate you on your engagement. She is a fine girl. I trust that you will both be very happy. Please bring her to lunch with me this weekend. I think Claridge's is the place for such an occasion. Sunday would be the best day. It is a shame that their trio does not play at lunch-time on Sunday, but no mind of that. One-fifteen p.m. I think would be the convenient time.

I walk slowly these days and the Oratory is a good distance from Davies Street. I had intended to ask you both what you would have for a wedding present. Here is advance notice of the question. Have you anything particular in mind? I had thought to give you the small Gainsborough that had been in our family since it was painted. Would this be a suitable gift, or is there something else that you would have?

Nephew, I expect your mother will be deliriously happy. I will telephone her when I finish this note. Your sister, well, she has already been hot on the line, a moment or two after I put down the receiver from speaking to you. What a woman – she has a compelling instinct to interfere in the affairs of others. Take no notice of her, Nephew. Seldom have I come across such bitterness, and in her case, bitterness without reason. Her fiancé then came on the line with advice and predictions. Always that young man is making predictions. I cannot make him out. Does he incite me so that in anger I may correct him and reveal some secret, or is the young man motivated by little more than his overwhelming conceit? Who knows and, on reflection, who really cares?

In fairness, I have to admit that the man is often right, but that pair, they irritate me beyond endurance, for now they have ruined my letter of congratulations to you and your fiancée with their intrusive personalities.

I wish you well, Nephew. I know that you will succeed, much depends on you. In politics you have made a splendid start. Soon you will have a wife to support you.

Your loving Uncle

Dear Nephew

I am deeply sorry to hear of the unfortunate conversation between you and your mother. She passed little of its content to me; from what I have heard you were probably right in your attitude to the matter of your younger sister. Nephew, it is not always clever to be right, as you will learn. To insist that another person accepts that you are right is certainly not clever in any circumstances, and in the matter of your sister it achieved nothing more than causing your mother a great deal of unhappiness, which I am certain was not your intention. Generally, it is far better that you spell out your views exactly, leaving the person you debate with in no doubt as to how you feel about a matter. Far better that they know how strongly you feel at the beginning, rather than have to guess after the end of a debate.

You, my dear Nephew, explained to your mother neither your views on your younger sister's conduct, nor how bitterly you resent the way that she has behaved. Had you done so, your mother might have agreed with you. I suppose that she has much the same feelings about that poor girl as you. Simply, you made the most terrible of errors when you faced your mother with your decision. A brief description of how you intend to treat your sister in the future and a long argument over whether or not you are justified in taking this action has not been helpful; it will serve little purpose and is a difficult position to retreat from should you find that the circumstances of your sister's life during the last year are not as you believe them to be.

Your mother is now, Nephew, deeply hurt. She has, I am certain you know, been counting on you to reconcile her with your younger sister; more than that, she was expecting you to rescue that child from the hell where she has chosen to dwell.

Nephew, I cannot accept your reasons. To tell me that your friends advise you to distance yourself from your sister, to tell me that they advise you that this course of action will be to the advantage of your political career, makes it no more acceptable to me.

I am, Nephew, an apparatchik who has in a lifetime of servitude to a political party seen worse than the actions of your sister. I have seen those who would dump a friend quicker than you would dump her. You are a politician, this you know. I believe that one day you will become great. This event will be but a barnacle on your skin, a skin encrusted with barnacles, the better to protect you from the staves of those who would strike you down.

Nephew, you take the wrong advice from the wrong people and you are about to take the wrong course of action. To tell these friends – who, incidentally, I regard as no more than a bunch of hangers on, squatting in your mind, searching for thoughts to make their own – was an error; to tell any group was an error. You might as well have published the story in the newspapers. I have already been asked of it by the vice-chairman responsible for candidates. One of the Whips, a man of Welsh extraction, drew it to his attention, a man I knew in my office when he worked there. He wished to enter Parliament, to become, you might suppose, a Cabinet minister or leader of a party; though his intellect should have disbarred him from success, his cunning assured him of it. No, he desired no Cabinet post, just the Whips' office. For heaven's sake, why? I asked the Welshman. I long to know the private lives of my colleagues, he said, and so he does, and uses the detail of them without scruple.

Now you, dear Nephew, are part of his repertoire. The activities of your younger sister are a tale that he will tell, should you oppose his will. I knew this man, I know him now, and often I wonder how a youth that was a joke should become an adult so full of bile, with such a certain touch in the placing and the timing of his evil.

Fear not, Nephew, for in your ignorance you have found the antidote for this man's poison. The story of your sister, now it is out, must be widely known, and quickly, before you are tested at the polls, for if others tell that tale they can twist it to your disadvantage. Told by you it will bring you only sympathy. As for your younger sister, I weep for her; she is but a pawn's pawn, in a game she knows nothing of, and if she did would have no part in.

I have taken the action that is necessary. I have written the required words and I ask no agreement. This is how it is to be done. Leave London by Thursday. I have arranged for you to go with a fact-finding mission to what was once the Soviet Union. Wear the clothes of a serious man, clothes that a man would use for his work; listen only, speak not at all, and if asked of your sister, say, in sadness, I have nothing to add, and if I had, this place of tragedy where so many suffer is not the forum for me to discuss the problems of my own family. On your return, the matter will be finished, the cartridge in the Welshman's magazine spent, empty, worthless – but beware, he watches you, for he can see your strength, he has heard you talk of principle, of a politics based on morality. It is to him as holy water to the devil: he will not try to break you or cajole you with flattery. He will set out to destroy you while young, to keep you from office. He is not mistaken, for those who can conduct the affairs of a government are many, those who know how those affairs should be framed are few.

You, Nephew, are a thinker, and politicians hate thinkers. Businessmen dislike them as well, and as for the public, they live in terror of those with ideas. You will, Nephew, need to be cunning in how you promote yourself. As for the Welshman, he is on the wrong track: when he sniffs after her it is the wrong tale that he tells. Leave him to me. I will set about pruning his roots.

I, dear Nephew, will have to do what I can for your sister. I shall see her soon, and this time not from a distance. I must talk to her. I know not what I can do at this time, but I pray that I can help the girl.

Nephew, I was called to the PM last night. He cannot understand these strikes. He believed the trade unions neutered, their powers taken from them long before he came to office. He does not realize that he, almost alone, is the architect of their current return to popularity. As one union is satisfied, another makes demands. They are like a nest full of young fledgling thrushes; no sooner is one beak filled than another pushes into its place.

The unions are not alone in causing the PM distress. His backbenchers troop into the Whips' office with demands for this or that. The place has become like a bazaar, with all the swapping and trading that goes on there. The poor PM thought that when he took office all would obey his every command. Now, elected leader of his party, twice winner of an election, all question every command that the wretched man issues; no sooner has he said do this or that than those who surround him suggest variations on these themes, threatening to bring him down if he refuses their demands, and so he threatens in turn to bring down his own government if they do not obey. The result, confusion. No winners, no losers, just confusion and a slide towards a general election. He decides to call an election and changes his mind because he has not the courage. He decides to battle on but has not the courage, all is confusion. He tells half his party one thing, the other half the other. He tries desperately to tell each the words he believes each will wish to hear.

Your Uncle

PS I am told there will be an election soon, an announcement next week. The party is in confusion, we will most probably lose the election – a sadness, but every sadness has its compensation: within a year we will lose our leader, the Prime Minister. Oh what pure pleasure to be rid of that joyless man; there is a successor who quietly waits – more of this when we meet.

Dear Nephew

An election four weeks from today, and no doubt you will have observed what stand the various journals are already taking on this event. One or two claim to reserve judgement, only, I assure you, because they feel that the public will be more impressed with their calls to vote for the party of their choice if they do not appear to have made up their minds until nearer Polling Day. Do not be taken in, they know full well whom they will support, indeed they have known for some years.

Nothing has changed, or, rather, on the surface nothing has changed, but to those whose lot it is to deal in these matters this time there is a discernible difference. The Opposition's papers are more confident, they scent victory. Our supporters fear defeat, our supporters in the Press would like to want us back in power but there is a hesitation, we have not given them the ammunition, we have not argued our case. We must help our supporters justify their choice of us; so far we have failed to do that.

Early days, you say, and early days they are, for campaigns do not go off like firecrackers, rather they smoulder and explode in the last ten days. Our situation would not matter if we realized exactly how we are situated. Not a bit of it, the PM believes that we are set for victory, believes in the power of his own oratory. Why, you may well ask? Well, those around him never cease to assure him of it. He spent most of the morning trying out different styles of soap box.

The public are tired of us and we appear tired to them. We need a freshness that we do not have, a freshness based on the past, using the past as a springboard not as a scapegoat.

Nephew, how on earth is it that a fact so clear to the electorate is invisible to our leaders? They watch their colleagues assessing each word other colleagues utter and take as evidence only the words that support their own prejudices. The public want work, wealth and safety, they wish to be cured when they are sick, secure when they are old, and more than all these things they wish to be proud of the country that they live in.

Nephew, they will have their revenge, and the irony of it all is that the PM will blame my office. Lack of funds, or lack of organization, or for that matter both. He and his circle will sit and debate an election that is past. Blaming the economy which they shaped, they will, however, pass over that fact, blaming the world economy while ignoring the fact that half the world has prospered while the other half has become so self-involved that it did not see disaster staring it in the face. Now these useless men will blame the very disaster they ignored for their defeat. Never has there been a time in modern history when the politicians of the Western world were so in tune with each other and so out of tune with their electorates.

Nephew, perhaps I go too far; the campaign has its course to run, we cannot leave the auditorium after the overture guessing who will be murdered in the last act. Though, dear Nephew, I have the feeling that I have seen this opera before.

Next week we will have the candidates' conference. Why it is called that I do not know, for the candidates play, so far as I can tell, no part in it. We will meet and lunch after that conference at my club, then, dear boy, it is back to the constituency for you and to the office for me, to do battle. I have seen many campaigns, and I am lucky that most we won. Have I enjoyed them? I always feel a sense of guilt when I begin to enjoy an election campaign; there is too much at stake for fun.

For you, Nephew, it is just hard slog, walking, talking, adjusting policy to fit the views of those you speak to. Do not ease up, beat the cover right to the end, you do not know what votes are hiding in the streets you did not visit. Word at the office is that your constituency is well organized. Take a tip from me, do not interfere with your agent, let him get on with his job. By all accounts he knows it well. Leave the handling of personalities to him; he will have his preferences, those he loves and those he hates. For yourself, smile at everybody. Even smile at your opponents, a quick smile, and forget them. Never mention them – tell the electorate what you will do for them and then tell them of the awful consequence of electing any other party. Give the candidates of other parties a brief smile, perhaps a handshake, no more is necessary. Do not make the mistake of lacking manners.

I attend meetings all day, checking this, checking that. The buffoon in charge of the Party's public relations insists on briefing the PM. He makes a total muddle of the opinion polls. I suppose the fellow is trying to give the PM good news when there is only bad available. In any event, he is a complete incompetent but, as is the way with these things, no one says anything about that till it is too late. They keep him as a scapegoat, yet I would not trust him to serve well even in that capacity, the man's a pantaloon. Once we had a man of consequence in that job. He never pushed himself forward, fixed the outcome of meetings before they began and smoked the grandest of cigars, filling the room with smoke which ensured that those meetings did not last too long. Success applauded his efforts. Many wondered why, since he seemed not to try too hard. Well, the truth of the matter is that his career had been a training for that job. All who succeeded him understood one aspect of it, and some I am afraid no single aspect of it. He, by chance, had worked as a journalist, worked in television and had the wit to leave the advertising campaign to those who understood the matter.

As for the polls, in the bowels of the office lives one of the few people who ever really understood them. How polls work is unimportant; understanding that they only answer questions is all important. Understanding that you can frame a question to give you the answer you wish is the real secret. I attend at the office in the basement where the one who knows about 'these things' lives. He, by the way, has high hopes for your election, which is just as well, for if you fail, few others will succeed.

I spoke two days ago to your mother. She prays for your success. Success may mean much to you, but I cannot tell you how much more it means to her. Following in your father's footsteps is how she put it. I hope sincerely that will not be the case with your career.

I have to put the matter of your younger sister on one side till after the election. The operation with the Press went well – not much coverage, but enough to defuse any attack on you during your campaign. As a safeguard, I had your mother's solicitor threaten the newspaper where I leaked the story with a writ; that fact will be attached to the file. I doubt anyone will touch the story while a campaign goes on. There are so many other matters to write about. As to the future, we will deal with any attempt to damage your reputation as it occurs.

So, Nephew, the very best of luck. I go into yet another meeting. There is, it seems, trouble with the youth organization, a group seldom without trouble. They make their names that way – to make trouble as a member of that organization is now part of a career structure in this party. Gone are the days when those girls wore dresses tight cut above their bosoms, nipped at the waist and flared to below the knee; gone are the days when those boys wore Brylcreem on their hair, wore dinner jackets and narrow bow ties. The only trouble they were ever in then was the occasional kiss and cuddle in a car park after one of their dances.

Your Uncle

Dear Nephew

The election has officially started. I am frantically busy from six in the morning to well past midnight. From midday to late afternoon the minutes drag. Politics is about the beginning and the ending of days; as in some board game, the contestants push and shove for advantage on the early morning radio programmes. Each tries to set the agenda for the day, and the winner's words are picked up by the evening newspapers, tossed here and there by that night's television, headlined in the next day's heavy papers, splashed by the tabloids and, as the public reads of yesterday's battle over their toast and tea before setting off to earn their daily bread, the struggle for tomorrow has begun. Nephew, when you read the polls remember the events that influence the public are two days old before they have an effect, and another three days old before they appear typed on paper as a record of public opinion. The wit and wisdom of politics will not win the day, nor the words of politicians at the hustings, but rather the advice of the Press, which becomes the will of the people, as expressed at the polls. The Press itself follows the tide of opinion, ripples becoming waves. Timing, Nephew, is all in politics; a wave of opinion against you is of little consequence if there is no election.

You are surprised. Surely, you say, the newspapers reflect the opinions of the Press barons. That, to an extent, is true, but the Press barons like to sell newspapers even more than they like to place politicians in office. The Press barons, who are as a generality a lot cleverer than politicians, have discovered that they can have the financial success that comes from selling newspapers and the power that comes from helping a prime minister to office. How that is done is simple. They will sniff out the way that the people will vote, and encourage them. So in a strange way democracy works after all. The people get the masters they want, generally in a government they deserve; then they set about blaming that government, forgetting that only a few months before they elected them. Strangely, a profile of the faults of politicians who make up parliament, of their talents and of their backgrounds, almost exactly replicates the profile of their electorate.

Those politicians who are not of great intelligence generally make up for their lack of intellect with a superfluity of cunning. They know what these wicked barons are up to, so they keep at my office a man whose job it is to mislead the editors. The best of that breed is long gone. I have written of him. His talent was not, as you might imagine, an ability to understand government policy – to understand this government's policy requires a mind so contradictory that its owner would live his life in danger of commitment to an asylum by his sympathetic family. No, this man who talked to editors had an extraordinary ability to drink champagne. He drank champagne at breakfast, he drank it all morning, his lunch spread through the afternoon towards evening. Then he would sleep in that lazy part of the election day when we apparatchiks sat in our offices reading the day's papers – the racing columns rather than the politics – and dreamed of days gone by or yet to come. At night he rose and, as darkness approached, so he descended on Fleet Street, or what now passes by the name for that decimated street, its dungeons scattered about London. The champagne corks popped and he would place a word here, a word there. They call these men spin doctors for the spin that they would put on an idea; this man was no spin doctor, no trader of facts, no seller of second-rate snake oil. This man carried the words of the leader of his party. What this man told came to pass.

Nephew, there is a difference between an apparatchik such as I am and a politician such as you would be. You will meet the people and likely not know what they are thinking, you will speak to them of your ideas. I will watch the people and judge how they will think, then set about encouraging them or discouraging them in their views. I have only known one politician who could catch the mood that would come and then speak the words that made it come. In time I will teach you this art, for I have watched it well and noted carefully how it is done.

There is also the other sort, large men whose hair blows in the slipstream of their own oratory. They can move the emotions of a crowd, make them cry, make them cheer, but bullfighters and comedians also do that, make them laugh, make them rise up in anger. The actor's role is played with carefully cut words, and as he leaves the hall the crowd speaks of this man, but already they have forgotten his words. He remembers their applause, remembers how it feels; it is the sensation that he seeks, like pressing your foot on the accelerator of a very fast car. Pass by love, beware of love, especially beware of the love bestowed by the masses. Better they hate and respect you than love and pity you, for in the former is power with press barons, editors, journalists and your colleagues who will have been elected by those unknown people.

Learn that when you speak, people at first do not hear; speak simply, speak slowly, repeat what you would have them remember, repeat it often. Learn how to say these words, for oratory is a craft like carpentry: if the words are not well set up, the result will be failure. Oratory should not be used in all speeches, save it for the moment. Often you will speak to entertain – so, then, be entertaining; often you speak to thank, then make your words full of thanks; sometimes you speak to praise – well, then, make your words full of praise. When you speak to tell of your philosophy, your idea, when you speak to convert or reinforce opinion, that is, when you use oratory not for reaction in a hall but for reaction outside it, then you throw a pebble into the pond and watch its ripples run to the bank and bounce back again, turning the water into turbulence. Then, my Nephew, when you have done this, remember, take no pleasure from the effect that your words have caused. Hear no cheers, fear no criticisms. This is just one move in carving out your electoral position, not a sensation used to boost your ego, nor a toy for an idle mind to play with.

I remember once a politician of handsome visage, fine frame and long hair carefully groomed. He took me to task. 'Just like the First World War, here I have just returned from the blood and sweat of the trenches to find the staff officers with their neatly pressed uniforms and polished boots in their *châteaux* drinking champagne.' All present laughed. He liked all those present to laugh at his jokes. The politician wiped his eyes with a silk handkerchief and slipped it into the pocket of his tailored suit, he bade them farewell – 'I am off to the Front' – he picked up his green Barbour (it had the look of a flak jacket about it). Never underestimate the conceit of mankind, just remember that in politicians this conceit is more often on show.

Dear boy, we will have a new leader. You pressed me for a name when we dined, and I would not give you one. As you know, I am not in the business of giving names, of making leaders or destroying them. A hint perhaps when the Party loses, and then the Prime Minister loses.

Dear Nephew, I am able to report that your mother is well pleased by your words to her – in fact so well pleased that she remembered my birthday. She sent a book, not one that I care to read, indeed not one I can exchange, for she has cut the price out of it, or maybe it was a gift to her. No matter, it will shortly be a gift to another.

When this election is over, you and I must plan another campaign, the downfall of that appalling man who I am told your sister still intends to marry in the autumn. I have been asked to give her away. For heaven's sake, do you not know a young man whom we could ask to Italy with her for the summer? I have spoken to a friend about this matter. He is very experienced in the actions that turn women against men. He says forget young men, introduce her to men of a certain age. I believe that he says this because he has reached the time in his life when he appears to be most uncertain about his own age. He is, I am afraid, in two words, too old. Do you know anyone in their fifties? I have a candidate or two – not very exciting I am afraid, but steady.

My very best wishes to your mother, indeed send her my love. I am looking forward to lunch with her in three weeks. The appointment was made two months ago. We will, she tells me, eat at Fortnum and Mason, the Soda Fountain, pink and blue salads and cold cuts, perhaps a glass of white wine. I cannot wait.

Your Uncle

Dear Nephew

I enjoyed our lunch at my club after the candidates' conference, a haven of good fellowship in what for me at least has become an increasingly tiresome election campaign. Thank goodness we give politics a miss.

I imagine you felt the same way as I did about the PM's speech. How out of touch can a man get? That great multiple throne the Cabinet sat on cost the Party much, but with barely their heads showing they seemed like so many targets in a coconut shy. The Chairman intends to send this grotesque piece of equipment around the country to the various rallies that have been arranged – a worse waste of money I cannot imagine. As for money, well, it comes in quite well at the moment but we are still desperately short of funds. Nothing in that department seems to work properly, yet the treasurers troop in at nine-thirty, when in times past they were in with the dawn. The Chairman's secretary, a woman known for working the longest hours in the whole of my office, a woman who has seen the politicians reinvent the wheel every few years, more talented by far than those who compete in the uttering of words at meetings, sits silent, seldom asked for her opinion.

Words, I am sick of words just strung together to draw attention to their owner's presence. Late at night we meet to chew over that day's news, while the media writes the news for tomorrow. The director of publicity sits late, desperately trying to convince us that defeat is in reality victory. Indifferent to the thoughts of the electorate, he believes these words. He serves this rubbish up for our consumption, and as he speaks editors all over London put to bed an assessment of our party, and still we talk to each other. I do not despair, Nephew, I never despair, my work is to serve. Win or lose, I shall still offer my views and obey the commands of my masters. I shall be at my office with the dawn, waiting for those who brief the ones who brief the PM, attending on the Chairman, at the beck and call of Cabinet ministers who shuffle their papers to give themselves time to remember which day it is and what town they are in.

My dear Nephew, I have made an enquiry as to the supply of posters to your constituency. I am told that our office is not much impressed by the efforts of your workers in putting these posters up. I am told you reply that the other parties pull them down. Well, pull theirs down and then they will have their work cut out putting their own back up and will leave yours alone. A better alternative, it seems to me, would be to put your posters where they cannot easily be reached. You say you are short of workers, for they go to help other constituencies. I am delighted to hear that, dear boy. Do the best that you can, for you will get little help from us.

You complain that the Cabinet does not come and speak in your constituency. Dear boy, to my knowledge you have for the past few months complained about almost every word that the Cabinet has uttered. Your seat is considered safe; if you wish it to stay that way I suggest you manage without the help of the Cabinet. You tell me that the Chief Whip's appearance on television was not helpful. Why do you imagine that I need to know that? Of course his appearance was far from helpful, he was a disaster – that lady from Exeter tied him in knots on a subject where we have a cracking good case. He is not good with the public, which is possibly why he was made Chief Whip, for chief whips deal in messages delivered in whispers and then reported second-hand through newspapers. They are not spokesmen, they have no talent for that role. So how did he come to appear? Who allowed this to happen? Chief whips during the campaign are theoretically in charge of who appears and when they appear on the electric media. This man forgot that this

[83]

was only a nominal arrangement, and when the first opportunity to appear on a chat show came along he appointed
himself. To say that the result of his enthusiasm was a disaster
would underestimate the situation. Such are the problems of a
campaign.

No one is reliable, no matter how important they are, but
always remember this, Nephew: for every mistake we make,
thank God our opponent makes another. Never, ever underestimate the incompetence of a political opponent. Why do
they make mistakes? It is simple, when the outcome of an
election is wide open, then all go along with the party line;
when the outcome is certain, then those who do not care for
the party line set out to establish their own policies. The result
is that a fighting party becomes a rabble, and the electorate
more confused than ever before.

Your Uncle

Dear Nephew

Last night at ten we received a warning of the result, but we have been told such tales before. Annoying as it may seem to you, dear Nephew, most of them here still believed that we would win. Now already they select those to whom they will allocate the blame. The Prime Minister must make his way to Buckingham Palace, and as he leaves that place another car arrives, there is another prime minister. It all seems so orderly, so natural.

On Monday I will sort my post and make arrangements for the week, attend meetings, write briefs, give advice and listen as that advice is consigned to the waste bin. I will console our leader, encourage his opponents, tell the Chairman he must resign if he wishes to stand in the leadership contest that will now follow. It seems as if I had done it all a thousand times.

Dear Nephew, I wander, lose the point of writing, which is twofold. First, to offer my congratulations, you are now a Member of Parliament; secondly, to suggest that we lunch next Thursday. I suggest that we eat at Simpson's — we can lunch in peace there. I dread the sly commiserations that defeat brings.

Now, Nephew, it starts. Now is the time that this party must begin the hard business of proving itself fit for office. There will be battles over policy, but take no part in them, it is too soon. Conduct yourself with diffidence, stay well away from policy. Now is the time to prove yourself as a mechanic of politics. Nephew, you must be the one to whom men turn for the solving of practical problems. How to acquire this? How to have the use of that? An introduction here, a contact there, now is the time for you to serve, to be helpful to all. Forget about policies for a while, you will have little need of them. Do not consider promotion, become like a well used armchair, not a thing of sparkling beauty, just useful, comfortable, reliable, always the same. Spend your time in the House, use humour but do not acquire a reputation as a humorist, and above all, avoid wit. Humour, wit and energy are the stuff of life but not of politics; use them as a young man and you will be quickly noted. Your rise to success must be moderated, to happen at a leisurely pace. With early fame and success you will acquire enemies as a shaggy dog gathers burrs walking through a thicket, so smile often and always laugh at the jokes of others.

Dear Nephew, behind this scene construct your policies. Debate them with academics, never with your colleagues. Debate each day as an athlete works out, exercise your mind. Learn about life, meet as many men and women of different occupations as you can. You increased your majority against a trend, but do not relax, work as if you had no majority at all and must still win the seat. Make certain you encourage the workers of your constituency to greater activity. They must raise the money to pay your agent – do not risk losing him to a richer seat. It will be hard in opposition to raise money; help your workers in that undertaking. Be ferocious in the pursuit of the interests of your constituents. In your public profile you should be known but not remarked upon. Under no circumstances let men say, 'This man will be prime minister one day.' Avoid the Whips' Office, have little to do with them, never visit them for conversation or speak with them in the lobby, be pleasant but distant with them, vote often, always vote. There is in opposition little problem of voting with your party, particularly for you, for I can conceive of no proposition this new government is likely to put with which you will have any problem disagreeing.

I look forward to our lunch. We have much to talk of. Your mother by the way is ecstatic at your victory, but I suppose you know that already. She telephoned me within minutes of the announcement of the count and spent fully fifteen minutes crying, muttered a few words, then hung up. God bless her. She is a fine woman and she loves her son. I am to spend the weekend with her. She wishes to invite another guest, but I told her not – it is hard for her to understand how tired are those who have just fought a losing campaign. I suppose, Nephew, I should write several paragraphs to congratulate you on your victory. Consider all that should be said is said.

For winners like yourself I know well it all seems like running downhill. You will find the weekend empty, waiting for the telephone to ring, not knowing quite whom to call. Spend it in your constituency, take time to thank your workers, indeed, thank everyone you meet, there is no harm in thanking the same person several times. You cannot do too much thanking in politics, thanking is the lubricant that makes the passage to great positions so very much easier.

Dear Nephew, just one other point. You will, I am certain, rise to fame and power. Remember this: you will meet many men and women along the road. Some will do you good turns, some often give invaluable help, some will just be there, of no real consequence you may feel, although I assure you they will take a view to the contrary. Some will try to hinder your progress, some may even try to destroy you, but my dear Nephew, you must remember all of them, giving them all your time however busy you may be, and, what is more, giving each one of them full credit for a success that you may well regard as your own. Do other than this and they all will be enemies; do this, and with so many friends, some of your enemies will join their ranks, and as for the rest, they will hesitate in their attack on you.

Good luck, my dear Nephew. It is now five a.m. I cannot sleep, I need to rest. This Friday is a day that I have for some time put aside to search for your younger sister. I feel I have neglected her this last month. I must make contact with her.

Your Uncle

[87]

Dear Nephew

The election result was a disaster, and that is not an extravagant word to use as a description: it was a rout, nothing more, nothing less. The first days of the campaign indicated that this might be the case. Every man, woman and many of the children in this land knew what the outcome would be, but not those who run our party. The Prime Minister was told that he would win, that this was what the private polls showed – quite clearly, the psephologists claimed. I have never known a poll show anything quite clearly; polls are but a snap shot in time, a frame taken at random from the film of our existence. At best they answer the questions that they are asked; at worse they are completely meaningless. The polls speak in a strange tongue, and each interpreter of that tongue can put a different emphasis on their words.

Four weeks and two days ago the apparatchiks of my office decided to massage the polls to produce a result that they imagined would cheer a dispirited leader. A last-ditch manoeuvre conducted at the first ditch which failed miserably: the very success of this move brought about its failure.

Dear Nephew, let me not race ahead of history. Let me tell you this sorry tale step by step, as it was played out on the battlefield of a parliamentary election.

We sat at that meeting, cheered by this news. Those who were young and still keen because they believed victory already to be in our hands, and all unknown to the enemy – oh, what joy, they thought, wait and watch the humiliation of the other parties. The older men and women, who knew how little indeed they knew, kept their silence, smiling not to spoil the fun, smiling not with pleasure at the thought of victory but rather at the folly of their brash young colleagues. How easy it all seems when you have never fought an election before. The secret, our secret that no other men knew, was that C2 women in the marginals were strongly with us. Who? Why? You may well ask, I have no answer, for that is but an example of the rubbish that they talk at my office meetings, and I must tell you, very impressive it sounds there. Only half as impressive, however, as it sounds when repeated – in, of course, the strictest of confidence – from the tables of the Carlton Club to the bar of El Vino's.

Why, you ask, does it not reach the ears of the Press? Well, of course it does, but there is no one foolish enough to publish it. Not because the editors know it for rubbish – I doubt if they do; rather they know it to be a fact so unutterably boring that no one would read it.

So, bolstered with hope, we went our several ways. For some days the election failed to take off, the Opposition shadow-boxed, the government thought about campaigning, but most of them kept to their own constituencies.

The Prime Minister, he was deep in the business of conducting foreign affairs. He was seen on television clasping the hand of every socialist head of state that came within reach. Then, after this phoney war, wartime – that's what they call it, believe it or not, wartime – wartime starts with every Cabinet minister demanding to sit on the platform at the conference to launch the manifesto. A turgid work of great weight and little content, this spectacle was for all the world like the opening scene of the Muppet Show, only not so funny.

Then, like knights in search of the Holy Grail, they set out, they being the Cabinet, the junior ministers, the loyal backbenchers, the loonies from the back benches, the bores from the back benches, those who have hopes hung on an unwinnable seat, those who have never fought a seat, all their camp followers of special advisers and hangers on in search of fame and perhaps even fortune.

You, Nephew, know something of this fatuous period, for

you were a small part of it. You thought it great fun and regard me as out of touch with the public. I regarded it as quite ridiculous, and in the event appear to be rather more in line with the public's views than you. I and many others can often tell what the public wants, and what that public wants is largely irrelevant. The art of politics is leading the public, not following it, and in this election we ran and ran and never even caught up with the public, let alone led it. We seemed cursed. Nothing went the way we planned it. Ministers arrived late for briefings swearing that they were given the wrong timings. The chairman of the Select Committee on Industry intended to produce a report highly critical of the government in the second week of the campaign – he, incidentally, is also the chairman of the Twenty-two Committee, a man who should know better – and this he proceeded to do, for he no more likes the Prime Minister than the rest of the country.

Well, Nephew, there was a hell of a row. One of the Prime Minister's acolytes telephoned him from my office. The report comes out next week, and I have no doubt the new government will give time for it to be debated. What with half-witted industrialists increasing their salaries by a hundred times those most men earn, and Irish troublemakers, the whole affair was a nightmare. The Chief Whip – he should know better, but I have told you before never to underestimate the ambition or conceit of politicians – he thinks to lead our party, and I suppose believed it would advance his case if he appeared on television. He was, as I wrote to you, cut to pieces, and the Prime Minister, well, no one needed to cut him to pieces, he went to bits right at the beginning and could not be put back together again. The Chairman of the Party – a monument to self-control – sat back each morning calm as the sphinx, and by the evening not a hair of his head was out of place. Perhaps he wanted us to lose, everyone else did, and that, dear Nephew, is about the nub of it. You do not win elections – call out all your own vote and you are in there with a fighting chance, but even that does not mean you will win. It is your opponent who decides to lose and fails to say the words that move their supporters to the polls. In this case we had without the shadow of a doubt decided to lose, and quite right we were, for now we can think it out again, decide on principles, decide on people and keep our policies mainly to ourselves until re-elected.

In the past few years, dear Nephew, we had the wrong people, too many policies and no principles, and early last Friday morning we paid the price. Thursday was quite a day in my office: junior staff despatched to help in constituencies, the senior figures taking to gossiping in each other's offices, studying the latest polls, searching for a grain of hope. A skeleton staff make tea and coffee, tidy the place, file documents and arrange chairs for the night's celebration; downstairs the media, upstairs the grand Party figures, most of whom have played no part in this election. Television cameras and their attendant trucks clutter the Square, crash barriers go up, police begin to assemble. The crowd arrive and mill around watching for celebrities. Spring darkness comes, the media's lights illuminate the crowds, our office is lit from pavement to coping stone, lights shine in the windows curtained only by mesh to catch the debris of threatened explosions. The media's cables clutter the pavements, the crowd waves Union Jacks, this building's flag waves back, and faces inquisitive of the noise outside peer from behind the window's flimsy covers – unpractised faces, to whom all of this is new; old hands read the sports columns of the *Evening Standard*. The crowd gathers, the Chairman arrives, the Treasurer's guests, the Party power-brokers, and all the while one room is locked and in it the psephologists who work the swings and predict results.

As the night went on, it became clear that events were not going the way our optimists expected, for no celebrities came to the Square. First the journalists left to drink Labour beer, sandwiches curled on their trays, sausages congealed in their dishes. Glasses stood in serried ranks, unused wine opened but untouched, nearly all had left. There remained one hack and his female friend acquired during the day, both past caring about winners or losers, their attention concentrated on a bottle of Scotch. The television cameras were long gone to their stations outside the Opposition's headquarters. Men coiled their black cables, loading them on lorries. The Treasurer's guests left, there were no crowds to hinder them leaving. The lights disappeared from windows. The Party barons settled in for the night. Champagne went undrunk. Whisky became our tipple. No prime minister came to thank and be thanked, no waving from the Chairman's window, no speech from the stairs, no crowd of wet-eyed typists, no drunken hacks. 'What will be their majority?' was the question sent to the psephologists for an answer. 'Large,' came back the reply.

When your vote breaks in a general election, the numbers against you multiply; it seems as if all luck is gone. I sat and watched television, the furniture vans' arrival in Downing Street. 'Rotten luck,' were our words to the Prime Minister, when they should have been, 'You fool, you brought all this on yourself,' but we were ever trimmers for that is our trade. Find a way through, take the convenient path, we were his creatures and will be the creatures of his successor, whom we, as is the tradition, will call 'leader'. I hope we serve him better but I doubt if we will, for we are the tools of his trade. We serve as we are asked to serve. We serve with alacrity and blame in the same style. The next day I cleaned the office. In a few weeks we will clean the Party.

Your Uncle

Dear Nephew

We're in Opposition again! For my part, rather a relief. I am rid of the civil servants who have made such a nuisance of themselves for the last four years, getting between me and my masters, monitoring and often frustrating the best advice that I gave. They are gone, and good riddance to them.

Never a day goes by without some politician, shadows of their former selves, coming in to ask for help, or help dressed up as advice. So many of their requests begin, 'Could you please advise me?' and end as a request for an assistant, an office or just the cost of a few bottles of alcohol. They are truly in our hands, the apparatchiks of my office are having their day. There is little these politicians can do without our help. The political advisers, too, have fallen on hard times, back on Party salaries with precious little to advise about, crammed five to a room in the Research Department, making their own tea. Now I advise them just what they may and may not do – few will last the course of a period in Opposition.

Poor dears, they know so very little of politics, these ignorant young fellows who were formerly cast in grand roles advising ministers. They had their hour, these little gods, putting words in the ears of greater gods. Not any longer. Now they are in the heat of a political battle trying each day to score a trick, and then the next day to score another. They are having to learn the art of politics without the time to study. It's a hard and tough world where you have to make a little go a long way, second-guessing a minister briefed by the might of the state, now they work for his shadow, always coming second, never making news, always having to comment but never having the last word. These children and their elder brothers and sisters must break out of this cycle and try to carve a place in the public's mind for their thoughts and

[93]

philosophies. Those men and women who call themselves politicians, who never had a thought or philosophy in all the time that they were in power. A sharp brain and an agile tongue are the least of the talents they will need if they are to make a mark in Opposition. My Nephew, just you wait, it will not take them many weeks to settle in their new roles. You will see that the quicker witted amongst them will realize that it is a deal easier to be reported if you criticize your own party than if you criticize your opponent's party.

Well, Nephew, the next few weeks will be a rough and tumble, then the summer recess, a bad time for oppositions. No opposition has ever done better in the polls than the government during the summer, except once, when our party were in Opposition and we at Party Headquarters ran a summer campaign unfettered by politicians and their minions – whose talent, I may say, if they have one, is for finding reasons not to take a sensible action. We moved to the enemies' ground, fought him at his heartland, and won. Generally, however, a government has all the cards. Governments make the news, oppositions comment on the news, then the summer ends with all the parties having conferences. The party in government can announce this or that policy to the cheers of its supporters. The Opposition can do little but try to restrain its more eccentric members from making fools of themselves and their party. We will both be at that great event. How will it go? Not well, I'll be bound.

Now we are coming to the *pièce de résistance* of this God-forsaken year, more entertaining by far than general elections or party conferences – a leadership challenge. There will be one, I have heard that already; they will deny it, but all the same they have laid their plans. He will go, of course, he cannot win. What has yet to be decided is who is to succeed him. Not the one who stands against him in the first round, that is quite certain. Never were the words, 'He who wields the sword shall not inherit the throne' more true than in our party these days. They are far too cunning to run their man in the first round. They have to be careful, however, for there was a time when the stalking horse won and stayed there three terms. They were sick as parrots, 'the men in grey suits' – a phrase, Nephew, taken from the world of journalism, misquoted and used in politics. It should read 'the suits' or 'financial controllers', not that it matters, the mentality of the suits and the grey suits is not dissimilar. No, they will not run their man first off, their candidate will be pressed to service in the second round, hailed as the hero who will unite the Party. He will, of course, do exactly the reverse. Let us pray that their plans go wrong and we by chance end up with a leader of principle and that his or her principles are right-wing.

Your Uncle

Dear Nephew

I am sorry to hear that your engagement is broken off. How sad this must be for all concerned. Far better to realize the problems at the beginning than to allow the momentum of events carry you into a situation that you bitterly regret.

When I was your age I made a mistake. If it is of comfort to you, my mistake far outweighed your own. An easy one to make, impossible to remedy. Should I live with that mistake or the shadow of the action taken – that was my dilemma. In the event, my mistake was removed by forces beyond my control. The evidence of the mistake lives on and is both a joy and a terror to me.

My boy, in time you will find a partner and you will marry. I wish you well.

Your loving Uncle

Dear Nephew

Do not imagine that I do not understand your attitude to your younger sister. I understand the position you take only too well. I have seen politicians behave in this way only too often. A whiff of scandal and they run a mile. Friendships are thrown to the winds, colleagues thrown to the Press. Those who tell quietly the secrets of others imagine that, in telling the Press about the failings of their colleagues, they receive some form of inoculation that makes them immune to criticism from those same journalists, should they fail themselves.

How foolish they are. Their treachery does nothing of the sort. There is no immunity to be gained by telling tales. Dear Nephew, I have seen men shun other men at their weakest moments when in their prime they would have rushed across a room to buy those same men a drink.

Nephew, you are not one of those, you are a man not to be shunned, nor one to shun those in trouble. Loyalty, Nephew, is something that you understand. I know this, for we have spoken often of it. You know that what starts as a blessing becomes a curse, always used to force a man to do something that he has no wish to do. Loyalty is not the issue here, and if it were, lack of it would not be why you reject your sister.

No, Nephew, you take your stance on the matter of your sister for other reasons. You can see neither the right nor the wrong of her position with clarity, and that worries you greatly. You can divine no reason for her actions, the way she behaves is for you totally without explanation. This frightens you, for you fear there is a streak of irrationality in your character as well and that you could behave in a similar fashion. It is not the fear of scandal involving your sister that haunts you; no, Nephew, it is the fear of a scandal involving yourself. You put the girl aside when she needs help, not out of cruelty but because you know not what to do about her situation. I say this, Nephew, if you cannot find a moral course of action in dealing with the affairs of your family, how will you ever find such a course when dealing with the affairs of your country?

Nephew, I tell you I deplore your attitude. You cannot cast this girl out, she exists. Life, if it is anything, is about other people. Mental surgery can rid you of the guilt but you will always bear the scar of that surgery. Nephew, I can and will help you in this matter, for you are not meant to be perfect. All I advise is that your attitude is neither practical nor, for that matter, necessary. You will, however hard you try, wrestle with this problem of your sister – far more, I may say, than that poor girl worries about her own situation. This will always be the flaw in your life, the flaw that makes you vulnerable. Nephew, the help I will give you, what form will that take? What is that help? I will connive with you in your self-deception. I will not speak of your sister to you, only in my letters will I tell the tale of the tragic child I have. A child at your request now unknown to you, introduced for a short time into your life, to serve my purpose because of my frailty. To preserve my conceit. A stranger you met, knew and who is now again a stranger, have no fear.

Nephew, we spoke of your maiden speech. You are in Opposition, you must oppose. Let it be short, let it be stylish. Show in it the true nature of the Party that you belong to. Put a little loyalty into the mix, for there is little that our Party values more than overt loyalty. This speech of yours does not have to be a manifesto for your life's work. Hide carefully in it thoughts now out of context without great meaning but about which, when referred to in time, men will say, 'Ah, he always believed that.' It will impress them mightily, for if there is anything that your Party loves more than loyalty it is consistency.

Nephew, I am sure your speech will be a minor triumph.

You worry about it; you fear failure, long for success. To the rest of us that speech will be but one stop in a career. Who cares if you falter? Your party has just suffered a severe defeat. Your leader fears for his position, the nation is about to be turned upside down by the new incumbents of a dozen ministries, and we have neither the wit nor the ideas to stop that tragedy. Your speech will pass unmarked, possibly unnoticed, certainly unreported. Fear not, dear boy, for the commodity that you have in plenty is time. Pace yourself. Always pace yourself. Life is like tennis, and politics particularly so: hit, bounce, hit, bounce. Nephew, we are still bouncing.

Your Uncle

Dear Nephew

Your speech went down very well. No one speaks of it. Now is the time to make friends, so be spare with your opinions. Take long hours to think on your philosophy, then in difficult moments the work will have been done, decisions will come easily to you. Each night as you prepare for sleep, Nephew, thank the Good Lord for the lack of decisions that faced you that day. Even government, when you come to it, is largely about carrying out the wishes of others, although the decision that faces you then will be whose wishes to obey.

When you lead a party, you will imagine that the members of that party will follow you. Not a bit of it. No flock of easy sheep, a political party, rather a ravaging pack of dogs who snap at your ankles and bite your hand, that is a political party. A desperate group of people, who try to divide their leaders. You will have many choices when you become prime minister. You surely will have no fear of that – it is the only matter that you need not fear. Should you reach that office you will find each day that your time is spent choosing between a number of alternatives – none of which is really attractive to you. Do not despair, Nephew, those eventful days are still a long way off. For now, build foundations of thought for the future – foundations of friendship for the future. And as for the future itself, never speak of it. (Never speak evil of anyone.) The future for you is too important to risk the pleasure of idle boasting, or the delivery of well-deserved insults.

From now on, Nephew, I shall call your elder sister as if she were your only sister, just plain sister. The other shall be, simply, the girl. Friend John I shall continue to refer to, with all the contempt I feel for that young man, as friend John.

The girl – I saw her last night. I tried to speak to her. She made no sense, her eyes stared at me as if detached from her brain. She saw an old man; she did not see me. I spoke to her – she must have heard a voice, for, turning, she turned back towards me. I reached for her arm and she pulled away. I had a grip on her coat, but it was torn from my hand. I could barely see the man who dragged her after him. She was not unwilling in following him, jut unsteady. Had he not pulled her, she would have fallen. I heard him curse, I thought I heard her sob. Her left arm trailed as if I still held her woollen sleeve by its cuff, and in her hand I saw that she held, balled tight, a handkerchief. I stood and looked first at one face, and then another, as people pushed around me. The bright lights of hot neon burnt my eye, yellows, greens, blues. Nephew, the girl was gone. I called, and realized how people stared, the crowd breaking like a river at a snag. A policeman forged his way towards me. I turned and hurriedly made away.

When I wrote, Nephew, of those politicians who fly at the scent of trouble, I should perhaps have mentioned another kind, such a kind as your father was. Politicians who are attracted to danger as moths to a neon light. Not physical danger, although often they sought that too, but rather a danger that could threaten their careers. Unnecessary danger that would hound them all their lives, which often they would flirt with, displaying a terrible hubris. Your father was one of those. We were alike as young men, neither one of us fully realizing the dangers that we sought. We played with danger as we grew old, he the rash old politician, me the ageing apparatchik. I fell by the wayside in our competition. He played those games till the end.

Dear Nephew, please give my love to your mother when you see her at the weekend. Tell her I shall ring as usual on Sunday morning. As for your sister, I saw her last week. She has accumulated a deal of fat on her face. Why on earth, when she comes to visit me in the office, must she bring friend John? I believe she has no wish to see me, it is friend John who wishes to make contacts on the stairway there. He lurks like the Ancient Mariner, with just that elderly sailor's persistence. The chief agent spoke well of him after such a brief meeting. I put the man right, and a deal of pleasure it gave me.

Your Uncle

Dear Nephew

There will be no battle to dismiss the leader of our party. No public battle at least. In private our leader has kicked, screamed, scratched and sworn at those who first suggested that he might depart. Three times the executive committee of the Twenty-two have been to see him. I am surprised that the matter is not already public. In truth, I suppose no one much cares what happens to him or even to this party.

Nephew, it is all about arithmetic: he no longer has the numbers, so he will go. This is not a case of philosophies competing with each other. You well know that it is an impossibility to discover what the man stands for, as I am afraid is the case with almost all those who would have his job. This party is short on talent and empty of ideas, tired, worn out, weakened by the loss of nearly half of its parliamentary members. In the provinces you would need to beat 'a county' to make a gathering of this Party's supporters. Few can remember the like of it.

So, what of those numbers that I wrote of? The electorate that chooses our leaders is so reduced, anything can happen. Well, Nephew, I can tell you, four years in the wilderness, then power if we are lucky, although in truth luck has little to do with it. The hard slog of Opposition is the training ground for power, the questioning of what we stood for and the ability to articulate what we now stand for. We must learn these things and, having learnt them, have the will to implement them. We must conquer fear, win the confidence of the electorate by explaining to them what we will do. If we ride out this period in Opposition in the hope that the government will make a fatal slip, we will be three terms at least without power. Nephew, we must be like that stone tossed into a lake, making only a small splash but with the ripples of our ideas heading ever outward till they become a wave to reach the shores of our electorate.

Nephew, I digress. At last the leader gave way to those who pressed for his resignation. The change will happen as it so often used to happen in our party – suddenly and quietly. The date for the announcement of this change is the day after tomorrow. There are those who would rather it had happened yesterday, minutes after the man agreed to go. They do not trust him. However, the papers are signed, and even he would find it hard to go back on this agreement. I am not party to what the man was promised – in the end he seemed to have no alternative. I suppose they know some detail that he would rather have kept secret than continue to lead this party.

I saw the leader soon to become the ex-leader yesterday. He sent for me not long after the assassins from the Twenty-two left his office. He railed and raved – the man is extremely bitter. What did I think, he asked? I lied, and I loved every moment of it. How badly treated you have been, I told him, quite disgusting the way the Party have dealt with you. Then I felt an urge to make mischief. Why did you give in to them? Why did you not fight them publicly, you have the voluntary party behind you? At least, Nephew, this is what that appalling man has always claimed. In his reply, without a moment's hesitation, he told me this. 'It is my health. For some time I have been sick, that is why I asked to see you. Will you please draft a statement to that effect, yes, an illness, nothing too serious. Say that I have given much to the Party but now I pay the price of ill health as a consequence of long hours. Suggest that if I rest, I will recover. In time the Lords, but at a time to suit my party – make it clear that I have been promised the Lords. Promised a position that is my right by a bunch of thugs who cannot deliver such a promise. There will be no peerages while this lot are in power. They will abolish the House of Lords before I get there.'

Nephew, he went on to explain that he is determined to be an earl, that is his right. He has earned it, he only did it for his family, for his wife. I could barely contain my laughter, for if ever a man were self-seeking it is this man. As we spoke the door kept opening. His secretary had quite a crowd in her office — speech-writers, geniuses of one kind or another, political advisers, the flotsam and jetsam that accumulates around power, checking to see if the power was still there. When the power moves, so will they, leaving a lonely man to answer his own phone, scribble his own letters — a man alone.

Our leader had by now drunk several neat whiskies, one after the other. I never thought that the man drank. I suppose I should be tolerant of someone whose career appeared from nowhere like a missile launched from a vessel on the ocean's bed, flying ever upwards, uncertain of its purpose, to disintegrate in the stratosphere leaving nothing of consequence behind, just the wreck of a party. This man should be famous, for he surely had the touch that turned gold to lead. His name should find a place in a dictionary, its meaning the converse of the Midas Touch. So much was given so easily to a man who set about destroying all of it while convinced that he knew how to make it all better. What a miserable man.

Seldom, Nephew, have I enjoyed myself so much as during yesterday's exchange. Delight, pure delight — he is gone, Nephew, gone.

Now, down to the business of a successor. The man that I spoke of will invite you to his rooms for a drink. Accept. You will be impressed. Tell your friends, show him to them. Move quietly, do not campaign openly, let this man make his case. He will do that well, for he is extremely able. I cannot commit his name to paper, I dare not write of him even to you; I am an official of this party. The Chairman has resigned, he intends to stand himself — well, that should add to the general frivolity of life. I will run the office, seeing that the children there do not engage in the fun and games that will go on across the road at the Houses of Parliament. You know the man that I write of, we have often talked of him.

Good luck, Nephew. Move quietly and with great care, trust no one – no matter how well you may know them. I will watch as the moguls of the Twenty-two canvas the voluntary party, canvas the peers, telling no one what the opinions of these men and women are. Then they will tell their colleagues in the Commons that the Party backs this one or that one, and amongst your colleagues, Nephew, you will find those who go on television to tell the world that their constituents back this one or that one because he will be a good leader and act in the best interests of their constituents. They flatter both those that elect them and he or she – for a woman may stand – who will offer them the best position when leader of our party. In the coming weeks, Nephew, you will see more hypocrisy practised than in all the years of your life. You will know it for what it is and you will hate it for what it is.

Hypocrisy and cynicism are not uniquely the stuff of politics nor indeed of politicians. These are the weapons used by the second-rate in all walks of life to destroy men and women of principle who would be true to philosophies that they believe will better the lot of the people they govern. Hypocrisy and cynicism are the tools of those who would only better their own positions. Those I write of have neither principle nor morals, so they cannot be chastised for what they do. Their evil lies in their success at thwarting the efforts of those who would bring about good government. They should be destroyed, Nephew, but I have found and you will find that they are of so little consequence that they are not worth destroying until, Nephew, they have their moment.

These next few weeks will be a time when such as I have described will prosper. Mark down their names, for you will clearly see them as they go about their churlish work.

I feel that I neglect the girl, but work here takes my time. I am consumed with the running of this office – all is chaos, no money, no talent. After the matter of our new leader is settled, I shall take two weeks holiday and I shall devote my time to helping the girl. Something must be done. I have written that before, but then I did not know what that something was.

Nephew, work hard and achieve the right result. Our party cannot afford the wrong leader. I spoke with your mother. Her conversation is now limited to your great success. The poor woman is obsessed with you.

God bless you.

Your Uncle

Dear Nephew

I have just met with our new leader, it was only a brief conversation. He is not the man we all thought him to be – loony is the word that comes to mind, prepare for fireworks. I have a meeting with him next week, at which he tells me I shall be instructed in his views. What a shame that my candidate turned out to be such a damp squib, he never even made the starting gate.

Now, out of nowhere, we have this new chap. The chief agent, protesting at the Party's lack of funds, told him that he could not be expected 'to make bricks without straw'. What did our new leader say to him? 'You are not expected to make bricks.' How on earth do you answer that? What a strange fellow.

Your Uncle

Dear Nephew

Whoever this man is who won, I am delighted, just because there is a change, any change. This man has slipped through to the surprise of all. They thought him useful to bring down the Party's leader. The power-brokers of the Twenty-two had no intention of him winning in the second round, but by the time he came to that second round this man was looking rather good. Still they damned him with faint praise, and sometimes with scorn that was far from faint, yet now he leads our party and a fine mess we are in. No chairman, no money, and enemies a plenty. More inside than out. He will appoint a chairman tomorrow, an inspired choice, a figure from the past, the distant past – even I was not around in his day. The Treasurer has resigned, and not before time I may say – a useless creature. Idle by nature and cack-handed as well. When he could gather himself together to do a day's work, the result was a disaster. The man upset more of our supporters than he pleased, far better that he was kept away from them.

A successor to the Treasurer, well, Nephew, that will be a hard post to fill, the way matters are at the moment. I would like to see it filled by a big man. A man of reputation known to be capable of thuggery on occasion, a man of private wealth, humour and connection. A man who knows how to entertain and does not hesitate to do so. To find such a man still active in business but with time to undertake the responsibility of raising the Party's funds, that is a different matter. We have a meeting of our new leader, the Chairman-to-be and myself to discuss this very matter. Have you by chance anyone to suggest?

I must cut this note short for I am pressed for time. There seems so much to do. Is it possible we are on our way back to power? I warned the leader of how the massed ranks of his enemies will try to bring him down, and his reply? 'Massed ranks? We will smash right through their middle, no compromise, no trimming, a direct and open attack. Our enemies will fall in behind us for we will lead them toward that they most desire, office.' I must confess, I found this impressive stuff.

Your Uncle

Dear Nephew

The new leader of our party is a most extraordinary man. I thought that I had the measure of him. I find that I hardly know him at all. Do you know that our leader takes cold baths every morning? He sits in the bath for twenty minutes surrounded by floating ice-cubes, the water he says must be around 14 degrees Celsius. When he gets out he tucks into a pair of kippers!

Yet the more time, Nephew, that I spend with our leader, the more I come to admire him. He has a sense of history and a sense of destiny – quite unlike his predecessor, who created economic woes as unnecessary as the Charge of the Light Brigade, and did it with less style. He is gone; God forbid that he return. His words have been discredited by his action. They will, I believe, be of little concern to those who direct our fortunes in the future.

Nephew, I put that man entirely out of my mind. I concentrate on the words of our new leader, who says that now our party is badly damaged we must tear it to shreds, and only then can we rebuild it. Our party must be a radical party, and so we must examine every aspect of our nation's daily life, and consider how each operation can be improved. Take law and order. I pointed out to him that it was my duty to explain how the electorate felt about law and order. I told our leader that no one believed that any party could do anything to improve the maintenance of law and order in our country. Our leader replied, 'That is unacceptable to me. Our policies will make the nation rich. We have a moral duty to see that our people enjoy the products of their wealth in safety: they will have a high standard of living and the freedom to choose, for freedom of choice without wealth to enable you to make a choice is but a charade.' I agreed with his sentiments – in effect he believes in cigars for everyone – but how to implement them? I told our leader of the events in America, the near breakdown of law and order, the mobilization of the national guard and the failure of that mobilization, for the national guard will not fire on Americans even if they commit crime.

'I know these things well,' he replied. 'But take the moral view: if a man is encouraged by the state to own property, that state has a duty to protect his property.' Our leader paused, not to think, rather to allow his mind to come back to his words, for his mind seems always far in advance of them. Or perhaps for me to come to terms with the implications of what he had just said. I protested, 'But we have no army worth the name, they went towards paying for our national deficit under the last government, and what is left of it will go as a matter of principle under this one. How can we maintain civil order by force of arms?' 'Not by force of arms, by force of will, the first requisite of government is the will to achieve a particular end.'

The words our leader says are right, Nephew, it is the will to achieve a policy that brings about its implementation. Do not start on a policy if you have not the will to finish it, do not engage on a policy if you fear to fail, for the fear of failure is a self-fulfilling prophecy. Believe that you will succeed and others will in turn believe that you will succeed; then you will have success. Our leader continued with these words. 'We must examine crime, what causes it and who practises it, follow the money, examine who profits from crime. Take drugs, for instance, consider the amount of money made from drugs and who makes these profits and the actions that they take in the course of making these profits. Consider the needs of those who buy drugs to have the money to pay for them and how they got that money. Attack those that make the trading in drugs an industry rather than just a criminal activity.'

Our leader looked straight at me. 'Drugs and the taking of them are totally abhorrent to me, I cannot tell you how much I detest them. We must, however, examine whether we should make them legal, making them at the same time cheap, draining the profit out of them and using the money we save – money that was formerly spent on stopping their distribution and apprehending their distributors – on education and relief for addicts. Not an attitude popular with my right wing but a moral attitude: if you cannot reasonably stop a man's action, you can at least alleviate the results of that action and at the same time stop others profiting from that action.

'The problems that the Americans are suffering could be overcome by prosperity. We can create prosperity, we will create prosperity. For the while we are in Opposition, able to do little about anything. Now we must plan and take our plans apart, shred them to find the fault in them, for it will be hard to come to power and we must not under any circumstances come to power unprepared.'

I asked him what his views were about the destruction of the army. As you know, dear Nephew, we have now reached the point where three bureaucrats service each fighting soldier. 'We need an army,' he told me without a second's hesitation. 'Not a toy army for parades, a smart battalion or two for the honouring of foreign dignitaries – that is useless to us. We need a proper army that can fight at division strength, an army that can fight as an army, an army steeped in the regimental tradition.' I asked him if this army was to be used to control the population to ensure law and order. 'No, under no circumstances. These soldiers are for fighting, they must expect to be killed. That is their occupation. We will re-create the great regiments and loan our soldiers to other nations, we will fight their wars for them, and in return they will buy our produce.' What about the lawlessness of our land? 'That is the duty of our police force. We will show the political will to implement law and order. The police will undertake the practical task of implementing our policies. Prisons will be made into places that you will not wish to visit twice. Prisons will not be about reform, rather they will become a deterrent. The judiciary will have no choice in the matter of sentencing. Sentences will be fixed by Parliament. The police will be better paid, for law and order is a citizen's most valuable possession and must be well looked after. We will cast our laws in such a way that our citizens are protected by them. We must be tireless in the pursuit of the guilty, painstaking in the protection of the innocent.

'The army will be the best army; no expenses will be spared. When your nation has wealth, others will try to steal that wealth. We live in times of peace. It was not always so, it will not always be so. Strength brings peace – weakness only war. We have a moral duty to the people, having given them wealth, to give them the means to protect their collective wealth and individually to protect their wealth for them.'

The platitudes of a conventional hard-liner, but our leader is a man of strong will. For my part, I pray that in time he comes to power. 'These,' he admitted to me, 'are primitive thoughts, instincts if you will. We are lucky, for we are in Opposition. We have time to think about these matters, to discuss them, to reflect on them, to polish them, but not to trim or neuter them.'

He is right of course. Governments have to turn yesterday's thoughts into today's law; oppositions have time to build an armoury of considered policies. We talked long about law and order, but one sentence of our leader's stuck in my mind. 'Law and order is the issue that will win us power. It affects all other issues, and, make no mistake, all other issues affect law and order.'

As I walked home to my flat in Dolphin Square, there was a touch of early spring in the night air. The sky was clear and I watched the last planes as they slid towards London airport. I thought about our leader's words and how he delivers them.

He is a strange fellow – as he speaks there comes a look in his eyes, a look that goes past those to whom he speaks. At first I believed this look to be affectation; now, after only a week or two, I know it to be one of dedication. This man will surely come to power.

Nephew, each day all of us learn something. I have been at the heart of politics for many years. I am old, I have seen much for which I care little, some of it, when I think back, which I loathe. Just once in a while out of the mouth of a politician comes pure wisdom. So it was tonight. Wisdom, not because his words were particularly wise, but because of the quality of his belief in those words.

Nephew, I have this advice for you. If you aspire to lead our party, without the will to implement policies, even the most brilliant and carefully thought out policies are completely worthless. Without the will to have your way, you'll retreat as our last prime minister retreated, dealing with each problem as it arises. You will become a politician of convenience who seizes opportunities and, finding them less opportune than you expect, you will cast them aside in favour of better-looking alternatives, and in time you yourself will also be cast aside and remembered not at all.

Dear Nephew, I have neglected the girl. I have indulged my own enthusiasms and called them work. I have enjoyed late nights and early mornings, for I am caught up in this great crusade. This night I go to King's Cross to see if she is there patrolling the streets. I will soon have to change from a man who cares to a man who does. Still I do not have any real idea how I can help this poor child. I will write when I can.

Ho! Nephew, how busy my life has become. In Opposition the likes of myself are right at the heart of matters. How will we oppose this government? Following the words of our leader, we will take the policies on law and order and we will attack every issue along those lines: if it is the economy and the government propose some particular action, we will show

how this action affects law and order. For us, every policy will be designed to return order to this country and to ensure that the law is upheld. So we will begin our time in Opposition.

Dear Nephew, I have not seen your mother recently – give her my love. Your sister makes no mention of me to her, that cursed friend of hers, John, makes my life a misery. But even he is only an amateur in that respect, compared to the Junior Treasurer. All the time he calls for openness and democracy, when in truth secrecy and dictatorship are how you win elections. The leader should have sacked him when he became leader, but leaders cannot always take the actions that they would like to take, or indeed the actions that they should take.

Your Uncle

Dear Nephew

Yesterday there was a mother and father of a row in the office. The new leader spent the day there talking with his chairman and the heads of the departments. I am afraid that our office is now barely worth the name of office, and most certainly can no longer be called a 'political machine'. Perhaps I am too harsh, but it is a machine that has become extremely rusty, one where the cogs have all been sold and the levers become too frail to risk pulling them and changing gear.

I am afraid in the last four years of government our party organization lost staff and accumulated debts. It was inevitable I suppose – budgets were cut back and good men and women left, or were dismissed in the name of economy. A false economy, for as our machine was perceived to fail, so support for it failed also. Then once again budgets were reduced, staff left and our political situation grew worse, and as the political situation grew worse so our financial situation deteriorated and the gentleman appointed by the then prime minister to run the affairs of the office – a man from business lent to the party by a crony of the then prime minister – made further cuts. How strange it is that politicians have such admiration for those who succeed in business, and vice versa. This delusion explains a lot of the problems suffered by our nation. If there is a man who makes a better show of his ignorance than the politician who talks about business, it is the businessman who talks about politics.

The two trades are totally different. Each operates on a different time scale, each requires different talents. As for running a political office, for a start you should dispense with budgeting. A political office should raise as much money as it can – spend as little as it can, saving all for the moment when it makes the 'Big Push'. Money should be spent when there is the political necessity for spending. Then and only then should borrowing be entered into. At that moment debt does not matter, only winning, for there are no second prizes in the electoral contest. Money should not be spent according to a budget drawn up with regard to fiscal prudence. All that leads to is a solvent life in Opposition, and for the likes of me a life of ease and idleness, for those who give money a total waste of their hard-earned funds.

Let me explain, Nephew, why I advised our leader to get rid of budgets. First, if you encourage your staff to break those budgets then what is the point of them in the first place? And if you never break those budgets you fight your enemy with a handicap.

Secondly, a budget is the amount the director of the office agrees that a head of a department may spend. Budgeting is a way of allocating funds between departments. The head of each department will see to it that he never spends less, the director of the office that he never spends more. The result of this is that the pattern of spending becomes rigid – in a trade where rigidity is an obstruction, in a trade where you do not know where or when a political crisis will arise. Crisis can appear from calm, a crisis which you can turn into an election or a crisis which can force an election on you. Politicians need to plan for this morning, businessmen are trained to plan for the years ahead, which is why they applaud stable currencies (even though many make their money out of currency fluctuations), steady growth and fixed conditions of employment. Nephew, all this is why they often find comfort in socialism. Businessmen try to remove the uncertainties that affect their trade, politicians on the other hand thrive on uncertainty. A politician's work is carried out in the second half of the day, an industrialist's in the first half. Business is about activity in the freshness of the morning, politics is about dealing in the dark hours of night.

Our office, Nephew, has been run by businessmen who, finding money in short supply and the efforts of one treasurer failing, applying their logic, appointed two of them and, still having no success, appointed half a dozen of them. These businessmen produce accounts for the purpose, it seems to me, only of telling the enemy what we are doing. Indeed, to tell him exactly how badly we are doing it, to show the exact state of the Party's finances, for that is the purpose of accounts. These men have always produced accounts for they have, in running a business, a duty to do so. Nephew, old habits die hard, which in itself is not bad if you have the habits of the appropriate trade.

Our new leader is a politician, with a politician's habits. The treasurers all trooped in to see him and left, having resigned. The Party's board of management banged on his door with angry complaints. He sacked them too, everyone! I believe the truth is that the Party are greatly relieved by the outcome of these events. The leader then appointed a new treasurer, just one. A fine young chap whose opinions are close to his own, and already this man is out stomping the countryside. He shouts the praise of his leader and gives solid reasons to those he asks for money. He understands the need for a secure base and has appointed a retired brigadier to do his staff work. Every day he telephones constituency treasurers, every day he asks industrialists for money, not in a haphazard fashion, no, this brigadier plans it all meticulously. People are being asked to give who have not been approached for years, and already money has begun to flow again. Money, Nephew, as you will doubtless find out, is the oil that keeps the wheels of politics turning.

Nephew, as I mentioned there was a mother and father of a row here yesterday. The director of the office introduced the new leader to the Party faithful – the Party's legion of officials. I felt sorry for the poor fellow. The new leader sat with great patience listening to this man introduce him to many he knew rather better than the director of the office. He continued to sit patiently as the director of the office told him of his plans and the budgets for those plans. Then the leader said, 'I want no budgets – I want this office run competently, cheaply, and I want it ready to respond to political opportunity. I want my Opposition to be run competently, and when we are the government I want that government to be competent.' The director of the office then told him that he had got it all wrong and, to cut a long story short, the leader sacked him. Sent him packing there and then. He must have planned it, of course, for he replaced him by promotion within minutes. He appointed, as you will read shortly in the newspapers, an old hand. A man who knows the constituencies and the voluntary party, a man who understands how you can change the direction of events in politics. Our leader appointed this man general director and a competent young fellow his deputy. No longer does our office have a director lent to it from industry, the first worthwhile move that has been made here in years.

Dearest Nephew, I cannot tell you of the work schedule that our leader intends for himself. Suffice to say that when a leader works hard, his office works hard. We have a new director of communications who will handle our relationship with the Press. Thank the Good Lord for that, for in the years in office the communications department of the Party withered on the vine. Its duties became mundane, for the Prime Minister put his trust in civil servants, and each Cabinet minister had his own man. Then there were the political advisers paid as civil servants by the State, who soon began to think like civil servants. The daily tasks of those who worked in our research department became mundane. The best left for industry or to fight safe seats.

As for those political advisers – why a true politician needs political advice eludes me. If he cannot or will not spare the time to study the political dimension of what he says and the actions that his department takes, that minister should not have the job. He should retire and take up agriculture, an occupation where a philosophical attitude to the weather is all that is needed.

No, Nephew, in politics you make your own luck or create your own misfortune. If you are to succeed you must lead events, to follow them is to fail. Give our office work of little consequence to do and it will invent work of little consequence but great expense, which is where all funds were spent. We are a political machine, and we respond to being used by a politician; we are not civil servants, conscious of our objectivity, always careful not to make mistakes. We are seldom accurate in our assessments but seldom entirely wrong either. We take a wide view. A civil servant will take only a narrow view. We exist solely to put our party into power and to keep it there. Civil servants are there to serve whoever rules. They make pleasant company for prime ministers, they may even share the same political views as the Prime Minister but they do not understand our party, how it works, or even why – no, their advice as a result of their ignorance is likely to be wrong. By comparison we exist only to win.

Within weeks our leader will have an office that can help him to victory, unlike his predecessor's office which watched him wander towards defeat. Nephew, I am excited by what is happening here, it fills me with energy. I have again a job to do.

Your Uncle

Dear Nephew

I have just come from the leader's office. He has the most tiresome of women as his secretary. He inherited her, I am afraid. She is stupid, and that is only the half of it, she believes that she is a genius. I know of no person so able at thinking up reasons for not doing what she is asked to do. She makes an art out of her arguments over every issue. I hate the woman, I plot her downfall every day. I cannot understand how he tolerates her. There is a far better girl who works for the Chief Whip, a rather jolly girl, intelligent, a mine of information. The sort of woman who can say no in such a way as to make you feel that she has done you a considerable favour.

I am sorry, Nephew, I digress. This awful woman was never intended to be the subject of this letter. Nor indeed was the charming lady who runs the Whips' Office – enough of both of them.

The leader has just given the marching orders to the chairman of the policy unit. There is no place for that man in Opposition, nor his unit either. The new treasurer, a fine man, conveniently says that there is no question of paying these people so they must be discarded, and as they go, so go their policies. Who can criticize our leader for saving money when money needs to be saved? He has set about changing the emphasis of the Party's policies. Before they know it, those policies that were neglected will be much talked about, those they favoured forgotten.

Our leader told me today where he felt that we went wrong. I have meticulously recorded his words. Nephew, I now send them to you. I suggest you put this letter away carefully for I shall tell no other, nor will he, for the past is the past. Water that has gone under the mill will grind no corn.

He does not wish to make an issue of past mistakes, but if you are to put a matter to rights it is essential to know where you have gone wrong, so here you have it.

'We set out to give what indeed is the right of all – freedom. To allow those who would trade to do so freely, to allow them to keep the profits from that trade, to pass those profits without encumbrance to their heirs. We recognized that some would succeed, some would fail, that those who would succeed should enjoy the fruits of their success. With the new freedom that we gave them we also gave them the responsibility to help those who failed. It is true that charitable giving rose dramatically as the energetic, perhaps even the lucky, members of our society became rich. For most of them, that giving became a conceit, not a duty; for others, they devoted their energies to taking rather than giving. Then they took too much, and some of the worst offenders in this matter were our own politicians. They allowed themselves to become examples of greed rather than examples of restraint. They did not seem to understand the reason behind our policies. We trusted those who made money. We allowed them to keep their money to give away rather than taking their money for the state to give.

'The policy was not wrong. The mistake was that some of the people did not understand the policy, while others understood but abused it. I intend to continue to use that policy but I will not trust the people completely. I will incorporate in that policy a whole series of carrots and sticks. A man may make money without restriction. We will abolish any impediment to the making of money. Then will come the sticks. We will penalize greed, reward generosity. We will never be able to completely close the gap in wealth between those who direct and those who follow, and that gap should never be totally closed. Those who lead must have an incentive to take the kicks that are inherent in leading.

'Therefore, those who direct must be seen to behave with

justice to those who follow, and if there is profit to be had, then it must be shared. Shared in differing proportions, but none the less shared. If there is hardship, then that too must be shared. Undertakings, like fish, go bad first at the head, and leadership is the quality that we must encourage. All aspects of true leadership we must encourage.

'At each end of the social spectrum changes must be made. Opportunism must be stamped out, and the Nanny State must be abandoned, the nanny given her notice. The responsibility for her job devolves on those who will lead. The State will play the part of referee, becoming the friend and protector of the citizens, having only a duty. We must set out to see that men and women wish to work and, far more important, we must see that there is work for them to do. This is the policy that I will charge my new committee with putting flesh on, to make this policy work, to see how our tax and social system can be changed to accept this policy.

'Furthermore, we will strive for excellence. We will try on the basis of what I have just told you to create a society that admires excellence. We will try to destroy the society that we have today, which is jealous of excellence. By excellence, I make no difference between the craftsman or the opera singer. Each will be encouraged, but by their peers, not by the state.'

Nephew, I like these words, I enjoy this man, I admire his determination. I wonder, can these brave hopes and aspirations become reality? I would never dare ask him this question. However, as I rose to leave him, he waved me back to my seat, leaned towards me with his hands gripping the mahogany arms of the upright chair that he sat in. He stared at me, a frightening stare, a look that many might take for madness. 'You doubt if all this is possible, I can see that in your eyes. We will succeed if we have the will to succeed. Success is ours while our will lasts. When our will fails, all is lost.'

I have to finish now, dear Nephew. That man's words whirl in my head, each one of them produces a thousand thoughts.

Your Uncle

Dear Nephew

I saw the girl. I watched as she stood with two others. Twice men spoke to her from their cars, many times they drove slowly past her, she bending forward and smiling a lopsided smile. One of her companions stood and talked for a while to one of these men, then they drove off together. The street was busy. Women came, stood for a few minutes and then either joined men in their cars or wandered on towards the railway station. The girl made no real effort to join the men or follow her companions. She stood and stared at a point fixed in her imagination.

A man walked towards her. As he drew close he struck her cheek with the palm of his hand. She seemed not to notice. He spoke to her again, she did not reply, he hit her about her head, hard, sharp blows indiscriminately aimed. At first they had no visible effect, then the girl fell at his feet. I ran towards her shouting – the next moment I was on the ground, I landed heavily. I do not know who tripped me, perhaps I tripped myself. The girl was gone. I was winded, my elbows and palms torn by the roughness of the pavement. Blood rose where they were grazed. I stood, dizzy, sore.

Nephew, I am confused, I do not know what to do. I cannot go to the police. This matter is delicate, I have to handle it myself, but how I have not the faintest idea. Of one thing I am clear: the girl is not there of her own free will, I am certain of this. In a strange way, I'm relieved. This fact at least leaves me free to act, to help her escape from whatever captivity she is in. I must think of a plan to help her, but I have lost touch with her. I went to that street and she was not there. I went there again and there was no sign of her. I cannot go tonight for I have been tricked into entertaining your sister and friend John for dinner.

Do you really believe that they intend to marry? He is boorish and extremely tiresome; she as you must know is an extremely determined woman. Whatever it is that she believes necessary for her to have, your sister makes certain that she has. If only that young woman would spend as much time and energy considering whether she really needs all that she desires as she spends attaining her ends. I suppose that is not her nature, for she is a selfish, greedy woman consumed with jealousy. A woman who wants different homes and partners, pleasures and pastimes. A woman too lazy to show any real commitment to any single project. A woman who seems to jump from one to another, whose whole life seems nothing but change – but in reality she changes not at all, staying the same tiresome person, with all the disadvantages of her tiresome character. I, poor soul, have to dine with this woman tomorrow, to have her ask my advice at the beginning of the meal; then it will be my lot to sit for the rest of the meal listening to her telling me why my advice, asked for by her and freely given by me, is totally unsatisfactory.

Meanwhile friend John will sing a curious refrain, so trivial that a more active man than I would kick him firmly in his crutch. No, I will sit and listen, and in time the woman will come to the end of her critique, thank me most formally for dinner, advice and my company. She will write and thank me before the next day is out, for your sister is a stickler for formality, she can at least always be counted on to do the correct thing.

Your sister has never learned – though I, incidentally, have often told her (as I've told you) that in life, be it marital or political, it is not always clever to be right. Far better on the appropriate occasion to allow yourself to be thought of as wrong. Perhaps, Nephew, even admit to being wrong when you and almost all those who listened to the conversation know that you are right. But your sister has to be right, she knows when she is right, and she must tell all who will listen.

Nephew, I have not seen your mother for some weeks. I have been too busy to write to her. Give her my love when you see her at the weekend.

How goes your constituency? You spoke well in the Budget debate. A shame that so few listened to you. I am afraid it is the nature of your calling to be heard by few and to be reported not at all – easier by far to create an effect by criticizing your own side, Nephew, than by attacking your opponents. I read your speech in *Hansard*. It was a good speech, just the sort of speech a man in your position should make.

I have spoken to both the Party Chairman and the leader, and I have their agreement that you should sit on the committee that works on our policy for law and order. It will become a key committee as time moves on. You must make an impact there, for that appointment is a great opportunity for you to influence Party policy. A great opportunity for you to draw to yourself the attention of those who can help you in the future. I expect you will speak in the law and order debate at the next conference. Do not speak at the Central Council. Keep your powder dry for the tougher audience and more Press attention.

We will lunch next week to discuss some ideas that I have on that subject. Simpson's, I think.

Your Uncle

Dear Nephew

It has started. The fighting inside the Party. I am afraid your Law and Order Paper has set the cat among the pigeons. The *Guardian* have it. You will have seen the coverage that they gave it. You wonder how that paper came by a secret report? I gave it to them secretly – how else could I get our enemies to publicize our policies? Fine policies, they are, too. The editor of the *Guardian* hated them, our rank and file on the other hand loved them and, I may say, so did many of the other side's supporters as well.

That, Nephew, is what politics is about, converting the views of the voters. Never fear to use the enemy's own newspapers to do that with. If you search for voters to convert you will find them thin on the ground among the readership of the *Telegraph*. No, Nephew, the *Guardian* attacks us today, the *Mirror* tomorrow – and that is where we will win support for this policy from among those in the heartland of both parties.

This policy has the virtue that it will consolidate the vote that we call ours – that in itself should win an election. This policy will win votes from amongst the voters that our enemies believe to be theirs. It's a practical solution to the breakdown of law and order. We see it each day, we hear of little else. Violence leads the news bulletins – personal violence, national violence, international violence. Our police force are on the point of rebellion, our armed forces no longer an army. We still have regiments, fine regiments, perhaps even amongst the world's finest, but they totally lack the infrastructure to fight as an army. We no longer have divisions, there has been no manoeuvre at divisional strength for many years. No army, as I knew it, able to help in international disorder, to defend our shores. So reduced in numbers is our army now that our national security is threatened, terrorism has become an everyday event.

No, Nephew, this policy is a winner. It is a sound policy, it is a right policy, and when it helps us to power at an election we will implement the policy with conviction and with competence.

Meanwhile, Nephew, we have no election and there are those in our party hell bent on tearing this policy out by its roots. Well, the fact we have no election does not matter, we will deliver policies one after another – body blows to a squabbling government. As for dissent in our own party, our leader will take this policy on law and order and he will present it to the Party Conference, obtain their backing and then beat those who disagree about the head with it. He leads our party to implement the policies that he believes right, and he will implement them with the support of his party, no trimming, no hedging. His policies will have a feel of common-sense about them: in their morality they will be fair; in their fairness they will command support. With this support he will defeat first the weak members of our party and then our opponents at an election.

Our leader is pleased with your work on law and order, and he intends to appoint you to the Committee on Health. Nephew, when we come to power you will be at the heart of our policies. The beauty of the size of our last defeat is that, so small is our parliamentary party, great reforms can be made. Small our parliamentary party may be, but ahead of us I see a great victory, a victory over our opponents, who, grown large, have grown weak.

I enjoyed meeting your friend. She seemed a pleasant girl. I am afraid I was decidedly bottled when she collected you at tea-time from my club. I hope that she will forgive me. I do not wish to turn to a sour note but your sister is intolerable. She came the other evening to my flat. She came late and uninvited, I may say, bringing as usual friend John. First, she says whatever I have in mind to give to you she must have the same; then she spoke of 'the girl'. She has found out about her and is trying to make an issue of it. I have to say it, Nephew, your sister is as ugly in her character as she has become in her body, and as for that grasping wimp, friend John . . . it was all, Nephew, a most unpleasant experience. I told her that the issues she raised were not her business. However, Nephew, you know your sister.

Your Uncle

Dear Nephew

Your sister's wedding was pure torture. I can understand why your mother asked me to give her away, though I cannot say I relished the task. However, in a family sacrifices have to be made. An odd sight we looked, I am sure – your sister short and plump, myself tall and thin, having trouble organizing my legs. It was just as well that the congregation had their back to us as we walked down the aisle. You would not have seen us until we came near the altar.

The flowers were wonderful. I spotted your mother's hand in them. Nephew, she has always had a talent with flowers and matters of decoration. Some of my happiest moments have been spent in her garden, sitting with a glass of Macallan's watching her tidy a herbaceous border. The sun, the buzz of bees, butterflies and new-cut grass. The smells of summer and its long evenings.

As she worked, your mother and I talked of many things. Travels in far lands, our childhood and our parents. In memory, at least, much of our youth was spent travelling by boat. We missed our parents, they seldom came to our schools. The Easter holidays your mother and I spent together at the home of the headmaster of my school. A good man, he died ten years ago. I miss him, he was kind to us. Christmas in London at a hotel. Only in the summer did we travel to the East. I remember my homes – there were a dozen of them in as many years. The servants, the chauffeur-driven cars, the parties given by our friends as each summer we set out, as likely or not for a new home. Her lengthy goodbyes to boy-friends and adolescent love affairs.

It was, I think, the security of those summer evenings that I loved, just your mother and I sitting in her garden. All we really wanted of life were plants, flowers, the weather to grow them in, a garden and our conversation – stupid conversation really, but, Nephew, simple jokes that belonged to us.

Who on earth chose the wedding dress that sister of yours wore? Do not tell me she chose it herself, I am sure that I am right. I am sorry, Nephew, that my speech was so short. I have written to your mother offering apologies. I had, and indeed I still have, nothing to say about the couple which could be judged complimentary. The ushers were the worse form of yahoos that I have ever come across, and I may say that I have seen a few in my time – his friends, I have no doubt. His parents, do they run a scrap-metal yard?

I stood outside the In and Out Club waiting for a taxi and watched the guests leave. I felt such an intense dislike of all of them I took myself to my club and stayed there till it closed. There was not one attractive human being amongst the lot of them. Nephew, I feel quite ashamed of myself. I should have escorted your mother out to dinner. I just could not face the rest of the day and dinner with the bridegroom's family. I made an excuse, I could not tell her the truth, I pretended that I had food poisoning. This was a mistake, as she wished to complain to the club's secretary. The bridegroom's uncle, it seems, is a member of the In and Out. He arranged the party there and took her complaining all very badly. He had a commission in the Reserve but you would imagine that by suggesting that I had been poisoned at his club I was insulting the entire British army. I did not mention to him that both your father and I had been in the Guards. I left anyway. I hope your mother will forgive me.

I caught a taxi, and as we turned into Trafalgar Square a car with the bride and bridegroom came alongside. They spotted me, so they began waving and shouting. Their friends in the cars behind joined them in their cacophony, shouting and pointing. I could have died of shame.

Your Uncle

Dear Nephew

We must fight hard for your paper on law and order. Your role is to explain, expound, argue with force, but do not attack the members of our party who oppose your ideas. A strange collection of individuals they may be, but they are members of the party to which we both belong. Resist the temptation of your agile tongue, do not ridicule them for their strange looks or boring habits – it is easy to do, but it will do neither you nor your ideas the least piece of good. On the contrary, you may by chance win, for you have the support of the leadership, but that victory will be a pyrrhic one – that victory will mark the beginnings of a long series of defeats for you.

No, Nephew, our case for reforms to bring about law and order must be fought and won by the power of argument alone. I will use a sporting analogy – you know how I hate sport, but nevertheless here it is: it is easy to kick the ball through your own goal, far harder to score at the expense of your opponents. I may have used this analogy before, but those words exactly fit the occasion. Nephew, your reputation must be based on how you damage your opponents across the floors of the House, not on how you damage those that sit around you.

My role, Nephew, is very different. I move in the sewers of politics, cajoling, persuading, leaking a thing here or there to the Press. Keep yourself clear of all this, Nephew, ready for the great battle on the floor of the conference. I will see to it that the right speakers support us. That in itself is a subtle art, and I know one who is an expert in it. I will have a meal with him at the right time.

The conferences you know from your experience were those under the leadership of that man whom we called leader, and who failed to lead us. No speaker opposed the platform at those conferences. Party unity, he called for, and none allowed to dissent – and what were we unified behind? If that man knew, he never told us. Still he demanded our support for his faceless policies. Support for him, what on earth was the reason for that? I can support a man who expresses views I agree with, attack a man whose views I disagree with, but the idea of supporting a man of no real views is to me detestable. This man imposed public loyalty and created a private treachery, for his dictate meant that respectable views that should have had an airing became the worst form of secret treachery. This was a man who, in his attempts to resolve his own insecurity, began an oppression within his party that if the nation had not thrown him out, would have become an oppression across the land.

No, Nephew, never underestimate the value of a fiery critic. They can be the most useful of creatures. A man attacked who defends himself against crude assault begins to gather popular support. A man who crudely assaults a subtle argument is lost.

Nephew, I will arrange the speakers. The motion will be critical. The proposer's speech will be boring – he has the time to bore for he proposes. Then a woman will oppose the motion and, speaking in favour of your paper, will play for sympathy. After this, a series of violent and really rather bad speeches will be made against your paper. I know those who make such speeches. They long to speak and can be relied upon to frighten any audience. At first they will be well received, then the hall will tire of their repetitious rhetoric, then an elder statesman who will show the merits of the woman's speech will call for moderation, after that a witty speech supporting the motion, then an emotional one. Finally will come your lord and master the Shadow Home Secretary. He will get by, at first. Then he will be barracked and finally listened to in silence. He will not get a standing ovation but the Press will respond well to his words, write of the support in the Party for his policies, in fact generally speak rather well of him. Not for his words, rather because they like him. The vast majority of our supporters do not attend conferences but they do read newspapers. You, Nephew, will deliver the *coup de grâce*. You will speak at a fringe meeting, a small but select audience, where your words will be well received. Later that evening you will join me and some of the more entertaining members of the Press for oysters and champagne in my quarters. The leader will not be there, but the Shadow Home Secretary will.

So, Nephew, you shall have your policy before Christmas, and as sure as Christmas comes the Shadow Home Secretary will send for you and ask for changes – small changes that must be made at once, he will tell you. Nephew, always beware those words 'at once', never be forced to agree in a hurry. There is no such thing as a hurry, hurry is the enemy of deep thought. Do not ever take the risk of acting on instinct when thought is available. Why should you be asked to decide in a hurry only to compensate for the idleness of others? Nephew, have nothing to do with hurry. In any case, what is this Shadow Home Secretary but one who aspires to great office should his party attain power? Humour the man, but not at the expense of your policy.

Dear boy, what will you do during the summer? I had thought to go to Italy but matters with the girl are bad. I watch her most nights. I have made contact with a friend of hers, a pleasant woman with a comfortable flat. I talk often with her. Yes, I answer your question before you ask it. I pay the woman. Nephew, it is a friendship that we have. You do not believe that. I need her friendship to be better able to help the girl. I think I will spend long weekends with your mother. I enjoy her company. However, you might, if you can, tell her in the most tactful way that I do not enjoy the company of her friends, an extremely tedious bunch. And under no circumstances do I wish to spend time with your sister and that bore her husband, who I now have reason to believe may be a rather sinister character. You laugh – well you may, for you do not know men as I know men, he is most demanding with his claims on her behalf.

Will you visit your mother or will you travel? I hear the Whips are looking for members who wish to visit Australia and Indonesia on a parliamentary delegation. If that is your wish, it can be arranged. Let me know soonest how you feel – perhaps next year we will travel Italy together.

Your Uncle

Dear Nephew

For me, Nephew, the summer has been an unsatisfactory affair. I loved my days with your mother, then, just as I was becoming used to the idle life of a good book, a glass of Macallan's and the hum of the working bee, your sister like some evil fairy in the Christmas panto arrives. What a strident woman that ungainly girl has become. Never subtle, she is incessant in her pursuit of the greatest gain. Her husband – what a pest he is. He came bearing news of every latest twist and turn in the political scramble. The left of the Party were engaged in cluttering up Tuscany during the day and removing Italy's contribution to the European wine lake at night, while the right slaughtered birds all summer somewhere north of Yorkshire. As he, thank God, is not the sort of man who would be invited to either gathering, where on earth did he get his information? Information, moreover, that as far as I can judge is probably accurate.

There will be strikes this winter. There will be inflation again, for inflation is not a monster that can be slain, or for that matter kept in chains, but rather a beast that needs domestication and then turning to the aid of our economy. A beast that must work for us, not a wild beast set to destroy us. Controlled, kept at a useful level, a spur to make the idle and timid invest their funds, to force them to take risks. A beast to be kept at a level slightly below that of one's competitors, to be used to bring a semblance of equality to our people, to give the opportunity to more people, changing dramatically their lifestyle.

That man presses me all the time, he never lets up, what can he want? We are, after all, the Opposition. Then we had it, your sister told me, her husband wants a seat – I fixed it for you, I must fix it for him, she says. Oh, dear me, how far from the truth that tiresome woman is. I cannot fix seats, I can barely help. I have nothing, only advice to give, and the wretched woman has never taken that before and I doubt she will take it now.

They left your mother's home in blind fury, leaving behind only a strong smell of sulphur, I could swear to it. But that was not the end of the matter, for from then onward they were in and out of your mother's house like a cuckoo in and out of its clock, always pressuring, always cajoling, and underlying all this a sinister threat. The rain came down in sheets. The glasses of Macallan's were more frequent and larger. The bees, sodden, returned to some hive; they were then not to be seen all summer long. The weeds grew in the garden, your mother fussed about the house. The heads of the roses, still buds, stayed tight shut and, with the humid heat, bent and rotted.

In London the girl vanished. I regularly visited my inform-ant. We sat in her flat, a squalid place in reality. Its true awfulness at first was hidden in my joy at finding a messenger – a messenger who soon would take my words to the girl and who, in the meantime, brought news to me of her welfare. I lay in the arms of this messenger as the rain fell outside. I smelt foul flesh, the bitter scent of artificial stimulants to pleasure. I lay in a room decorated with the trappings of my messenger's trade. They hung like trophies on her walls. Nephew, I am desolate there is no news of the girl. Day after day all summer, no news, Nephew, I despair. I shall forsake this false messenger. Why should I visit her? She has nothing for me. No words to tell me, nothing.

Nephew, when I go to the Conference I will travel to Brighton by train. Will you come with me? I go on Sunday afternoon.

Your Uncle

Dear Nephew

I was delighted to receive your letter, to read that you are safely returned from your adventures in the East. I am interested, I suppose, that you enjoyed your time in Hong Kong. I have very little regard for that place – far too many people, far too little culture, all buildings of no consequence, the streets filled with humanity. If that is not complaint enough, the weather is unbearable for a large part of the year, a city with the air sucked from it.

I was sorry, Nephew, to hear of your débâcle with the airline that brought you home. Do not fall into the trap of believing that because you are a member of Parliament all will treat you with deference. You may think you are a cut above, but few others will regard you as more than a charlatan at best, a crook at worse. I am surprised that your complaint to the airline was received with contumely, perhaps you went about it the wrong way. Nephew, when you complain, never start at the top, for to do that means you will be passed downwards until you give up in frustration at hearing the words, 'I have passed this matter to the executive responsible, he will deal with it, I have told him to give your complaint every attention.' No, Nephew, start at the bottom and work your way up, saying, 'I have spoken to your assistant and he says that only you can deal with this matter.' In time you reach a level that fears for your complaint to go higher.

Nephew, when you travel again, go to Italy where inefficiency is endemic, relax in the warm air, look at that country's masterpieces, and take insult and lying as a matter of course. You will probably live longer as a result, and certainly you will enjoy that life far more than if you worry, complain and pull rank on those who manage aeroplanes.

Your patient Uncle

Dear Nephew

I have just heard from our leader that he intends to reform his Shadow Cabinet after the Conference. He will see how they do, then make his judgements. Our leader has this idea: he will let all the talent in our Party 'have a go', as he puts it, at least for the next couple of years, then on the run-up to the election he will finally select a team to win.

Our leader tells me that you are to be included, not in the first rank at this stage, naturally, but included none the less. He has yet to decide on which portfolio you will have. He also spoke of a Party post. Congratulations, Nephew, you have earned your promotion, whatever that promotion may be.

The arrangements for your meeting at the Conference fringes are well in place – we have a room in the Conference centre itself. The room will hold several hundred and the acoustics are good. I have arranged that the meeting be held before the round of cocktail parties on the Thursday, shortly after the Shadow Chancellor finishes speaking. You will have a good audience and you can drive home the message of the Shadow Home Secretary. You may believe that the best of the fight will be over by then. I sincerely hope that it will be. What you have to do is clear matters up, tidy the issue package and seal it – a workmanlike job is what the Party needs. Choose your words carefully, for your reputation will be judged on the competence of your oratory. The Party must be reassured, not informed.

Still no news of the girl. I visited my messenger – I know I said that I would not, but I cannot take the risk that she knows something of the girl, that I through neglect might fail to collect that news from her. No news, but she gave me hope. There is word of the girl. She says nothing definite, but a woman she knows spoke of someone who sounds to me like the girl. The messenger will arrange for me to meet this woman. I will see both of them one evening the week after the Conference. The Monday evening it is arranged for. We will meet at the woman's apartment. I pray that she knows something.

Nephew, will you pick me up after lunch on Sunday, and we will take the three o'clock train to the Conference. I have invited for dinner two young men from the Research Department and a girl who seems to be a rising star – she will be deputy director of Communications soon. We will dine at English's, I have booked a table for eight o'clock.

I am worried about our director of Communications, a bright young man left over from the past regime. He does his job well but he does not have the background for it. The post demands a man who knows of television and wireless, perhaps a man who has worked in broadcasting, both in religious broadcasting or news and frivolous soaps. He should have worked as a journalist for a time. Certainly he should know editors and how to put a paper together. The role is not one that solely involves the telling of truth when convenient or the telling of lies when the truth is inconvenient, there is far more to it than that. This post seems to need a man who can draw attention to our views.

What our party needs is a man trusted by its leader who can listen to the actions that our politicians propose and then say, that way leads to popular disaster, this way leads to popular success. A guide is what we need, a wise friend who can tell his friends that we take the right road. A man who is capable of showing the self-evident truth of our Shadow Cabinet proposals. No magician practising black arts who makes lies seem truth, just a man who in telling the truth can make the people who communicate with the millions listen and believe.

The Conference seems set fair for success – however, that is where danger lurks, for humans are perverse creatures, and what seems successful they will often destroy, while failure they will often embrace. My God, Nephew, have we not had our fill of failure? Look around you at the empty Opposition benches as you question the PM. See the crowd that sits opposite you in the House, cramped on their benches, they squat in the aisles. We must change all that, and you must play a major part in that change.

Nephew, your friends are not the friends of war, to change the course of great events. They are frivolous friends. Convenient friends who, should they help you to high office, perhaps the highest office, will demand a price, a price that you may not care to pay. Distance yourself from them. I have written of these friends before, friends both inside and outside Parliament, friends who in the success which attends you seem like loyal supporters. Escape these friends, Nephew, escape them before their friendship becomes a habit and you become their slave.

Nephew, your mother is sad these days. Will you stay with her the weekend after the Conference? We can travel to her home together. She needs her family around her. I worry about her health, I feel that we are not told all. Oh, how successful our family is, yet we have such a potential for failure where love and consideration is in need.

Bring a copy of your speech with you on the train, we can run through it together. On a Sunday afternoon we should get a carriage to ourselves.

Your Uncle

Dear Nephew

My messenger's friend was of little use. I spent a pleasant evening with both of these women. I took them to dine at the Savoy. As for news of the girl, they had none. I was deeply disappointed. I cannot tell how I worry about the fate of the girl. They both promised to look out for her. I am sure it is only time before they have something. I spent the night at my messenger's flat. Her friend stayed with us. Do not worry, Nephew, these women do not even know my name. They do not know where I live, nor my occupation. I am sure that they are crucial to my search for the girl, for they move in the right circles. After all, Nephew, who else can I ask for help without taking the most enormous of risks? I must do all this for the girl's sake.

Nephew, I have news for you. I am deep in the confidence of our leader and he has told me that he intends for you to be in his Shadow Cabinet when he shuffles it the week after next.

You impressed him no end with your handling of the paper on law and order. 'Just the right balance in his speech,' was how he described your efforts at the fringe meeting. 'No hostages to fortune, no pandering to basic instincts, a speech of integrity filled with common sense, a rare commodity, strangely called common' – that is how he put it to me. You have touched a very strong cord in our leader, Nephew. He had a few kind words for me as well. I will not repeat them, for I do not care for immodest men.

Our leader intends more for you than either of us could have expected. He will make you the Shadow Minister with responsibility for Health and Social Security – you may pick the team that you will work with. The leader expects similar results of the same high standard that you have set with your paper on law and order, a difficult task, Nephew, and one that will be made no easier by your youth. I will put it about that, with such reduced numbers in Parliament, he was forced to jump a generation, and will say that this appointment is only temporary, in line with the leader's policy. Perhaps it is.

Dine with me next Thursday, I have some names that I would discuss with you. We may well lack numbers in the House but we have youthful enthusiasm aplenty outside of it. Soon, Nephew, you will be appointed to the Shadow Cabinet. Nephew, I congratulate you, for you have indeed excelled in your career. A fine promotion, your mother will be justly proud of you.

Yes, you must marry and provide an heir to carry on our family's name. Take your time, Nephew, but I am sure that you have made the right choice. Think of your career and time these matters well, for there is nothing like a wedding just before an election to put joy in the hearts of your electorate. Do not waste that opportunity, you need every vote that you can get.

Where will you spend Christmas? I suspect I will spend the holiday with your mother. No doubt I will have to put up with your sister – still she pesters me for a seat that her husband would be capable of winning. I dare not tell her that I can do little or nothing to help and that little, should I do it, would be done at a huge risk, not to me but to her husband himself, for the woman just would not believe me. So I say that I am working on the matter, I gave him a map with constituencies marked on it to see which he would rather have, and the foolish child your sister pops around to an estate agent with a list of safe and attractive seats just to test the availability of houses in those areas. I laughed till I cried – how long can I keep up this charade? They come to me, for they know that they have no alternative, his chances of selection are zero. He would do better just to apply. If I tell him this he will not believe me, and I cannot in truth give him the evidence that proves the selection committees of our party have selected far bigger dolts than him. Nephew, I need help in this matter. What a Christmas is in store for me.

Life here at the office is hectic. The Chairman is away, taking a short holiday after the Conference. On reflection, how do you think the Conference went? You could hardly call it a success, but in retrospect I have come to the conclusion that it was not the worst conference that we have had, by a long shot. I must say that our Shadow Cabinet have a lot to learn. Our leader's reforms have left the Party shaken, the massacre at the polls left it demolished. I have some suggestions for him; action must be taken, and taken speedily.

May I say that my suggestions involve you. I will not tell you of them, Nephew, it is too soon – not that I feel our leader will turn down my advice, far from it, he will almost certainly take it, and that advice is greatly to your benefit. Meantime, Nephew, distance yourself from those friends of whom I disapprove. One at least of them would use your success for his own ambition. You will, he hopes, become his footstool. Nephew, all these friends of yours would use you and pretend that they help you. Most of them you need not fear, but the one I have told you of is dangerous – I will not write his name, he is far too dangerous. This man you call your friend, who you believe will advance your career, is as treacherous as the Welshman.

Never, Nephew, was a man more mistaken than you, for this man will drink with you late, and while you take wine he takes only water. He will talk with you of trivialities, for that is all he knows of, taking in return from you information that you give in friendship, information not of itself vital or even important but, pieced together as this man pieces together the gossip of many men, this unwitting information of you and your like makes available for him a message of vital importance, that one day he will use to bring you down, and bring you down he surely will for that is his stock in trade. Minions he can promote, the fortunes of great men are beyond him except in one respect, his ability to plot and then to destroy them. Your friend will then skip away innocent, saying to all that it was the gods who performed his dirty task.

Your Uncle

BY HAND
URGENT AND EXTREMELY PRIVATE

Dear Nephew

The leader has taken my advice, you will hear from him in two days. You are to be appointed the chairman of the Research Department – that department is to have its own direction as once it did, it will work directly for the leader of the Party. The Chairman has agreed, indeed, he welcomes your appointment. At last that department will live again and no longer trail behind various outside organizations engaged in making the Party's policy.

You will be based at the office. I have arranged a desk and a room for you. The desk is a fine old thing at which eminent men once sat. The room the other side of mine from the Chairman has a fine view of the Square and its church. I shall see lots of you, Nephew. I cannot tell you of the pleasure that it will give me, having you work in this building. Can we dine the night that you hear the news? My club, a simple dinner with a Marie Jannet of Latour – I have a few of them still stored there. A useful bottle, a Marie Jannet, a magnum is too little for a pair at dinner, a second magnum by far too much, most of it must be wasted, and a series of single bottles embarrassing and a trouble for the wine butler. Remember, Nephew, that when a Marie Jannet is decanted few can tell it from a magnum.

We will dine and dine well, for the two of us have much to celebrate. This action of our leaders will be well received by the youth of our party.

Nephew, I was right, I am to spend Christmas with your mother. You I am told will spend it with friends – does that mean one friend in particular? Tell me when we meet.

Your Uncle

Dear Nephew

I write in haste, for I am about to leave for the Christmas break. I truly wish that you were to spend this Christmas at your mother's home. It has been such a fine year for you, to spend its closing together would have been wonderful.

In the matter of your friends, I fully understand your position but I would not have you jeopardize your future out of a sense of misplaced loyalty for those who will show no loyalty to you. I do now blame them for that – I have strong reservations about loyalty, far better that men follow a leader who inspires and leads them than follow another from a sense of loyalty. I have, Nephew, observed that it is only the weak and inadequate among leaders who frequently speak of loyalty and demand that emotion from their colleagues, often in petulant terms.

No, Nephew, the emotion that I admire is trust – that followers should have a trust in their leader's judgement, his ability to lead. Loyalty is a debt that must be paid for past favours, loyalty grows out of affection and is important when the object of this loyalty is no longer important. Loyalty is the commodity of the past, trust the commodity of the future.

This, Nephew, is the rub: you should not trust those friends of yours, for they have been deceitful with others. That is a fact. Deceit is a disease without cure; it can be suppressed but never dismissed. Deceit lurks in the soul only looking for an excuse to be released in order to carry out its grimy work. These friends of yours, because they are deceitful, will never trust you, and so, not trusting you, they will prepare a plot. Nephew, far better that you should dine with your enemies, for there lies honesty: they work for your downfall, but by knowing you and perhaps coming to like you they are weakened. When they take their knives to strike you down there is just a chance that they may hesitate, and in that hesitation lose all.

Nephew, do not resign from this club that your 'friends' have formed, that is too open a rebuke. Just fail to attend. Do that now, before your success becomes obvious, lest they accuse you then of grandeur, of having no time for them. The jealousy of these friends exists already, though they may not know it, and your success will fuel its flames. Fail and they will hail you a hero, promote you to positions of little consequence, and all the world will wonder how such a failure can be such a success.

These dining clubs, all of these associations where politicians gather in groups, are there for only one purpose, to promote the interests of their members – people of little or no consequence. Leaders, Nephews, do not need the help of such as these. Wise men see and follow a leader, fools will follow success.

Nephew, I have left a parcel with this note. I hope that you receive it safely. Your secretary has instructions to give it only into your hands and she has been warned that it is fragile. In fact a bottle of elderly whisky, 25-year-old Macallan's, it has had a good training in a sherry barrel and has a fine flavour as a result. It is a whisky that approaches a liqueur, and I hope it warms the holiday for you – not that you will be in need of warmth.

In any event a very happy Christmas, Nephew. Drink the health of your mother and myself, we will surely drink yours. As you set out enjoying your holiday, we will reminisce about the past and speculate about your future. By Boxing Day we will have made you prime minister and kept you in power for three terms at least.

God bless you and keep you, Nephew,

Your Uncle

PS I have news at last of the girl.

Dear Nephew

How was your Christmas? I shall not be back in the office
for a couple of weeks, I have work to do. I must confess that I
was a day late arriving at your mother's. Just as I finished
my note to you and had begun to tidy my effects ready for
departure, the telephone on my desk rang, the private line.
Few people have that number – the leader of our party, a
member or two of the Shadow Cabinet and several editors
who are our friends. It was my messenger. She has that
number as well. I thought it best to give it to her. Rest
assured, she does not know whom she rings. Nor where I
answer her calls from. She had news for me. Would I see her
and her friend as soon as I could? I went that very evening.
They have found the girl, they will arrange for us to meet
early in the New Year. This is why I shall be absent from the
office.

I have put this matter to one side for too long. Now I must
act. How will I act? I do not in truth know. How can I plan? I
have no evidence to base my plans on. I will break the habit of
a lifetime. I will rely on instinct and luck. I have no choice, I
cannot delay a moment longer. I await each day another call.
The messenger has my home number. I know that line is
secure. Intermediaries have to be paid. I told her to pay them,
to pay them whatever they asked. I gave her a considerable
sum. Her friend said that it would not be enough. I gave them
more, much more. I hope this time that the money is not
wasted. My money has been so often before. I worry about
the money. I worry about just the frustration of failing again
to contact the girl.

Dear Nephew, Christmas went as Christmases do. We ate,
we drank, we watched the Queen's speech. I cannot understand why each year we all have to be subjected to a public-

relations exercise on behalf of Africa's worst dictators. There they were, smiling and strutting around the gardens of Buck House as if they owned the place. Those monsters should not be allowed beyond the railings, let alone given the run of the palace. The sooner Britain leaves the Commonwealth and the Queen directs her splendid efforts exclusively on behalf of the British people, the better. The irony of all this is that these days we are no longer her subjects, just citizens of Europe, while the peoples oppressed by those awful monsters still are subjects of Her Majesty.

Well, that apart, she does her Christmas thing really rather well and it makes the most marvellous prelude to an afternoon nap – a nap that I most certainly did not get.

First your sister collared me to talk about her sister, the girl who, as she so sweetly puts it, has gone missing. She knows far more of all this than she is letting on. Her husband must have discovered something. I had the very strong impression that the girl is in touch with him. I suspect that your sister intends to use the girl as a means of forcing me, and perhaps you, to carry out her wishes. Your sister is a wicked woman, well matched in her choice of husband. She will use the girl against you, to threaten or embarrass you with her at an inconvenient moment. Mercifully, she does not know the whole tale, for the girl herself knows nothing of that. Only I, your mother and yourself have the truth – unless perhaps your mother has told the girl, but I doubt that, I cannot believe that she would, I cannot believe that she would have committed such a folly.

Nephew, leave all this to me, have nothing to do with any of it. I will see that matters end well, have no fear. You must have no involvement whatsoever with the girl. That, after all, was your wish. It could perhaps have been otherwise, now it is too late to change strategy.

Then, Nephew, having sent your sister off with kind words and talk of going to my room to change, your mother appears and demands a game of bridge. I lost £7.50 to your detestable brother-in-law, who plays cards really rather well. I left on the afternoon of Boxing Day to return to London pleading a grave political crisis that had to be coped with.

Your Uncle

Dear Nephew

I have met with the girl. She is in a bad state. I have rented an apartment for her. My messenger and her friend stay there with her, they try to bring that poor child back into the real world. I visit her as often as is possible. They think it better if the girl does not live with me for the moment. Although I do not understand their reasoning, it seems I have little alternative but to join in with their wishes.

Nephew, I was right, your brother-in-law had tracked her down. I cannot prove it, but I think he held her captive without her realizing this to be the case. The man is totally evil. I was wrong about your mother, she had told the girl the truth, so long hidden, that she was adopted. Did you suspect? I believe it was the sudden knowledge of the truth that was responsible for her irrational behaviour. She is a good girl, but now I find her almost a stranger. The messenger and her friend are good-hearted despite their sordid professions, I have of necessity been spending much of my time with them in the last week or two.

Nephew, I am perplexed about how to deal with this matter. I suppose in time I will forgive your mother. We have for years been close to each other but never have we discussed our problems or our emotional reactions to these problems. We have sought our own solutions, solving our problems each in our own way. We are of that generation. We have been close, we love each other more than most brothers and sisters. Your mother is a fine woman who has suffered greatly, and this latest episode with the girl must have caused her much grief. I fear she confided in your elder sister. I would not blame her. I will forgive her, but not yet.

Your sister and her husband are another matter – they are a danger to you, a very real danger, for they are consumed with jealousy. If your brother-in-law cannot have success in the world of politics your sister will try to ensure that you have only failure.

Beware, Nephew, success wins few friends. We have both ridden high for some time. Through you I expose myself – always before I was just another apparatchik, whom no one cared about. I carried out the commands of whoever commanded. Now many believe, wrongly, that I played a part in the coming to power of our new leader, and, rightly, that I am also the sponsor of your success. I am a player in your 'friends' game, and that game can only be played by their rules – so be it.

The next years bring only hard work, then the fight. I pray for victory so that we will govern. Next week Parliament reassembles. I have first thing on Tuesday a meeting with our leader, after which I will see you in our office. Then we can set about a moral reform of the system for providing the care for our nation's health.

Your Uncle

Dear Nephew

I write to you from Italy. The girl and I have spent Easter in Venice – what a city. I do not mean the paintings and buildings, though of course they are wonderful. However, all Italy has them. No, I mean the people and the way of life. The girl and I have walked till our shoe leather grew thin, talked till our voices were hoarse, we sat and ate tuna-fish sandwiches, drank the coffee of the bars that abound in that city. In the evenings we sat and took grappa in the squares. One day we were taken rowing. It was a Sunday and our host rowed himself, standing in his skiff's stern holding his oars crossed like scissors. He propelled us amongst the small sailing boats which, with their painted triangular sails, infest the lagoon on sunny weekends, carrying friends who picnic and fish, unaware of Italy's turbulent nature, free from the terrors of the world. The girl has begun to relax in my company.

Dear boy, I am in love. How I love that troublesome child. You have no idea how she has improved since I have sneaked her from the clutches of the messenger and her friend. I am afraid they are quite evil. The girl was their meal ticket and they expect to have her back. I will have to come to an accommodation with them, but it will not include the girl.

Our host rowed till near lunch-time and we landed on the tip of S. Erasmo, the isle that feeds Venice with its produce. We lunched in the Easter sunlight at a *trattoria*, taking our food at trestle tables set in the garden, sitting on iron chairs. Our host knew many who lunched there – what a party. The girl grew restless. She is not good in the company of others. I walked with her along S. Erasmo's only road, we turned into the fields and fell on our backs in the new grass, rolling and crushing the wildflowers with our bodies, tearing them up by the roots in handfuls, then laughing at each other and, laughing, we ran, turning and dodging till I held her tight to me.

I return in a few days. I have acquired a cottage on the banks of the Thames at Hammersmith. It has a large garden. The girl will live there – I will tell the messenger and her friend that she ran while we were in Italy. I shall be distraught and I shall dissemble wonderfully and take pleasure in doing so. I must keep the girl safe till she is fully recovered.

Nephew, I cannot tell you the joy it is to write to you. I seem to do that so infrequently now we are both working in the same building and see each other most days, sometimes several times a day, so that letters between us seem an irrelevance. We are closer than ever, but without the letters that we have written for many years we seem to drift apart.

Your Uncle

Dear Nephew

The girl and I have spent the first month of the recess at Hammersmith. She is making good progress, slowly she begins to meet people who come to our house. I tell them that she has just returned from travelling. If they press me, I say in America. Such a big place, and Europeans seldom venture past its great cities. I tell them that she has travelled in Arizona and Nebraska working for a family. I take great pleasure in concocting these lies, it has all become a game that the girl and I play. We choose our guests with care and then entertain them with our fantasies.

The messenger and her friend were furious when I told them that I had lost the girl in Italy. I offered to pay for them to go there to find her. They agreed at once, suggesting the last week in August to search the beaches of the Italian Riviera. They returned yesterday. I see them tomorrow for their report. I imagine their search will become an annual event. I enjoy playing with them quite as much as they seem to enjoy robbing me. I must, dear Nephew, admit that this strange game adds an excitement to my life that I have never experienced before. My games with these women stimulate me more than you can possibly imagine.

The girl and I work in the garden in my spare time, in the evenings we read. She is rather more intelligent than I gave her credit for.

Nephew, I have read your paper on the Health Service to be released officially just before the Party Conference. I will leak parts of it week by week till then. I believe that the *Daily Telegraph* is the place for this piece of policy. It is far too reasonable for the *Guardian*, and I doubt if they would give it much coverage. In any case, the *Telegraph* must applaud your ideas if we are to succeed in getting them made Party policy. I have talked to the leader, who is delighted with what you have produced. I can tell you, Nephew, that you will have rapid promotion to high office when we come to power.

Nephew, I have not spoken to your mother for months and I regret that. Always we have been very close, I am so sad about the rift between us. I wonder, Nephew, if there is anything that you could do to get us together again. I do wish that you would. I have heard that she is not at all well. Is there any truth in it? Your sister tells me not. Am I to believe her? My instinct says no.

Your Uncle

Dear Nephew

I hate to write this letter to you. I loved your mother. I am devastated at her death. There was no time for reconciliation between us and I shall live the rest of my life in the shadow of this unfinished business. How I regret the misunderstanding that forced us apart. How I regret my pride that kept us apart. How I regret the curious natures of your mother and myself, that gave us love for each other without the pleasure of telling each other so.

Nephew, there is little to be said. I comfort you in a moment of sorrow and say only this: when both the parents of a son are dead, only then is he truly a man responsible to himself for his actions. No one to share the blame or console the blamed.

No, my Nephew, you are alone. God bless you and keep you. Take heed of my mistakes when you marry and have children. I should counsel you to be at one with your sister, taking this moment to do that, but in truth I cannot come to terms with that woman.

Your Uncle

Dear Nephew

The summer weather as usual does its best to imitate its winter cousin. How different from the heat of Washington. My trip with the leader was interesting – Nephew, that is too small a word to describe time spent with that man, it was stimulating, riveting, it is not too much to say the English language does not have a word for his level of energy, his forceful intellect and the sense of danger that he creates around him.

We spoke at length about your Shadow ministry. The leader wants no scapegoats, he is not prepared to come to power by using scare stories of women who become pregnant to jump higher on the housing list or foreigners who come to Britain to get their teeth fixed. Of course there are abuses; wherever you have a system that gives money to the under-privileged, there will always be those who already have privilege in excess who try to grab some of that money. This is the nub of his policy. It is for you to address the problem of getting the money to those who need and deserve it. Ignore abuses of the existing scheme, do not waste time on finding a scheme that can never be abused. Pay particular attention to those at the margin of need and allow a safety belt for them – your solution must have a moral basis, a basis to be seen as fair, and capable of being demonstrated as such without effort or chicanery.

A strong and fair system of social services is the safeguard of capitalism. The old argument still holds good. Capitalism is the best way to create wealth, for a nation to earn the money that a nation needs to look after its poor and its needy. There can be no debate at this stage about that, the debate is about how the money is spent. If it is seen to be spent fairly on the poor and needy, then the system for its creation will not

[161]

come under attack. The electorate will not cause an outcry if individuals earn more, taxation will be lower and, strangely, the nation will be richer, for we will attract talent rather than frightening it from our shores. All of this, Nephew, is simple and has been well rehearsed by many politicians. Members of our party, however, are liable to deviate from the narrow path; they either wish to give too much to causes where they believe that giving will bring political acclaim, or make savage cuts that destroy our great institutions and the sense of history that our people have.

Next, Nephew, the leader has in mind for you and your Research Department to study employment. The moral basis of work. There is food for much thought there.

I leave London tomorrow. I travel with the girl across Italy, following our own inclinations. I am triumphant, Nephew, never has my life had more purpose. Never have I felt so in control of my destiny.

I received a letter from your sister on my return from Washington. I have left it on my hall table unopened till the summer is past. It can only contain trouble, and that trouble will just have to wait. I will not see you till the end of September, Nephew, write to me care of the Grand Hotel, Rome.

Your Uncle

Dear Nephew

I sit in the Commercial Hotel at Lucca. The rain comes down with the strength and shape of iron railings. I am seized with gloom. The girl lies on her bed and sobs. There is no consoling her. I do not for the life of me know what causes her grief. I ask her and get no reply. I ask again and she chokes on her words. Happiness, she claims, and still she cries. How dismal I feel, Nephew. Tired and dismal, no hope in me. The weather gives me the excuse not to move from this hotel yet. I have tired of the place and long to be somewhere else. Where that is to be, that is the rub.

I wrote to you, Nephew, when your mother died. I wrote about my sadness that she died before we could be reconciled. It was careless of me, for I made no mention of your grief, nor, I must admit, did I give it any thought. I apologize. I know how you must feel at the loss of your mother, I know that loneliness for I have felt it all my life.

My sister was a fine woman. She was proud of you, Nephew, you were the first and only opportunity in her life for true and justifiable pride. Her life was not an easy one, of that your father made sure. She, however, told no one, made no complaint, she was loyal to him. Nephew, see how dangerous is that word loyalty – that was her mistake, she came of a generation that used the word without thought of the consequences to their lives. Loyalty, Nephew, is the quality of princes, they dispense loyalty. My sister should have sent your father about his business.

Nephew, how sadness grips me. It is only as I write that I can loosen its grasp. Last night we wandered, the girl and I, wandered from church to church, through the amphitheatre where in daytime the market stalls stand, along the walls of Lucca, down streets, past palazzos, their walls quilted with faceted stone, squares and fountains. It seemed like another age. We had, I think, dined too well on pasta and roast hare. I know that we had drunk too much of the local grappa – our heads were hollow and our hearts were high. It was five in the morning before we made it to our beds. Sleep was like some stranger looking occasionally around the door jamb, who came with good intention but clumsily destroyed his own purpose. Now, Nephew, we pay the price.

I would say this of sadness: without it, what price is happiness? The man who knows no valley can never find a hilltop. The girl sleeps, the child cries no more.

God bless you and keep you, Nephew, and may he guard your mother's soul.

Your Uncle

Dear Nephew

Just a note to suggest that we meet for dinner the week before the Conference. I am told by your secretary that you will be home by then.

I did not know that you intended to travel with your young lady. Your secretary was at great pains to tell me that she was accompanied by her mother. I know her mother slightly – it can be little hardship to have her as part of your party. How wise you are. When will you announce the date of your wedding? My informant, your secretary, who succumbed only after considerable quantities of champagne, has told me more than perhaps she should. Do not reproach her – I am afraid that I tricked the poor girl, leading her to believe I knew of it all. In truth, I had guessed. I gather the end of next summer is to be the date. What a shame that you could not delay this adventure till just before an election. Everyone loves a wedding, there could be a thousand votes in it for you. Still, with the way we rise in the polls you will be safe enough and, barring accident, you will be part of a government. Perhaps not with a Cabinet position, that would be too much to hope for.

I met that ancient Welshman at the Beef Steak last week. You remember him, no doubt, though he is long gone from Parliament. What a devious man he is, his plots so complex I doubt if he understood them himself; he is still plotting, and he means no good to you or me. The Welshman spoke well of your brother-in-law, suggested I helped him to a seat. Never. I will not lift a finger to help that monster sit in Parliament. The Welshman had a grin about his chops. How he has aged, a combination of lack of alcohol and too many cigarettes has brought his body to the point of ruin. The man walks only with the help of sticks.

Your sister comes to see me tomorrow. I will not seal the envelope that contains this letter till I have met with her. You, Nephew, will have news of her latest nastiness.

Nephew, how right I was to hold this letter until I had met with your appalling sister. She came to my flat with her husband – happily she knows nothing of my home at Hammersmith, she still believes the girl to be at large in some urban jungle. She did the talking, her husband listened. 'Just when are you going to arrange the safe seat for my husband that you promised?' I prevaricated, mightily offered them tea and drink, used every device to avoid the issue. 'This has all gone on for far too long. We will not tolerate any further delays on your part.' Just how they are to tolerate or not my delaying that wretched man with his crude ideas achieving a position from where he could do a great deal of harm to our nation, I do not know. The husband may very well be clever, but he is a man without scruples, hand in glove with the Welshman and his chums, a power at any price man, and the price? That price has to be paid by the population in the end, and it is far too high. I will have no part in helping this man.

Then her husband passed a packet. She put it on the table. 'I wish you to look at these,' she commanded. 'Later,' I said. 'Perhaps tomorrow.' I knew, Nephew, full well what was in that packet. I had prepared myself for that, rehearsing it for years. I barely looked at the photographs. I knew how they would be. The girl with men, dressed and undressed. The girl with men, drunk and sober, tears staining her skin, or maybe that was my imagination. The girl laughing at the lewd acts of others and grinning with delight at her own. The girl stabbing her arm with a needle filled with poison, and then a series that showed her degradation as a result of that vile stuff, pictures of her past. Nephew, this was the stuff of her past. Her past is gone, the humiliation is over.

I, Nephew, was to be the messenger to tell you that her husband must have his seat or the girl will be exposed for who she is, and her connection with your family made much of. The exposure would be made worthwhile by the fame of your name: you would be damaged by virtue of your own success. Thousands of young women fall into the situation of the girl for one reason or another. Collectively, they are news; individually, they would not make a public hardened by exposure to crime and porn, both as fiction and fact, turn a page. This girl, thought to be the sister of a well connected young man, a member of Parliament known for his hard line on crime, a young man destined to become a famous man, would sit on the front page. Her real story would run for days – you are both too good-looking, and the media hungers for pictures of beautiful people. The great irony is that, were you a pair of hunchbacks, a paragraph or two is all that you would receive. I handed back the photographs and agreed to be her messenger.

Your Uncle

Dear Nephew

I cannot understand your actions. Why did you refuse to discuss the problem of your adopted sister after I wrote to you, putting me off, fixing a day far in the future, making an appointment that you had no intention of keeping, then agreeing to another date so that I could sit down with you and together we could decide how this was to be dealt with? We met, we lunched together, but there were others present, we dined in company. We walked between appointments. Always you refused to address this problem, always refusing to meet me, until a moment in your words 'when we will have time to think and to decide'.

Now I find that your brother-in-law has been selected for one of the safest seats in the country. I saw it all happening. At first I tried to put a stop to it, then I tried to speak to you about it. 'He's only on a selection list, they will not have him, there is a far better woman available,' you told me. You are right, she is far better, and also wrong, for they did select him. Do you know how he answered the question of how he saw his role in Parliament? 'I will carry out the will of God and my constituents.' He won by a mile. Who told him what to say, I wonder. Have you had more dealings with the man that you told me of?

Nephew, you were wrong. I never took the risk of letting him near a selection committee. You were wrong, or did you plan it all? Our meeting – well, there is no point in it now, but we shall meet, you and I, for there are matters that need resolving between us. You will travel to Brighton with me. We will go by car, and I will drive, so we can speak freely.

How did you like the piece in the *Telegraph* on Social Security? It paved the way for the publication of your policy document rather nicely, I thought. You will speak in the debate – the motion sets the scene well enough for you. I hope you agree, for I wrote it myself. The proposer is a sensible fellow and he is capable of making an extremely good speech. I hope that he does this time. This conference, Nephew, is the turning point. Now we must begin to prepare for an election any time in the next two years.

I will pick you up on Sunday after lunch – about three p.m. and we will set out for Brighton and to fame.

Your Uncle

Dear Nephew

You were tremendous – your speech cut new ground. Somehow you managed to take the Party with you. How you must have enjoyed that moment when the first applause smashed at you standing on the platform. You must have known that you had your audience in your hand to crush or to caress, and you did both. I am told that to make a speech like that is similar to driving a fast car, you put your foot on the accelerator and the car responds, the adrenalin runs in your veins, then at a whim, a carefully rehearsed whim I may say, you touch the brake, the car slides to a halt throwing your stomach against your chest – then off again.

Your applause ran for eight minutes, every man and woman on their feet. Luckily it stopped before it overtook the applause given to party leaders. Remember, Nephew, the friendships that you made in the hall with that speech are of a temporary nature. The enemies that you make caused by jealousy will endure well past the end of your career. That day, Nephew, you crafted your philosophy into a speech, and they loved it. Never fall into the trap of trying to find only ideas that they will love. Nephew, you have a future and a role in all our futures, you must remain always your own man.

Your Uncle

Dear Nephew

This is just a Christmas note to wish you well. Much happiness may you have.

The parcel to which the note is attached contains a cup that has been in our family for generations, made in London during the reign of Charles II. It bears our arms. I hope this silver goblet gives you much pleasure – I have used it often, and you must have seen me quaff the Macallan's from it. Now it is yours, as it should be. I hope that you will have a son to drink his whisky from it. I find old silver gives a special taste to whisky.

Many congratulations on your engagement. Your secretary was quite right, just before Christmas she said, just before Christmas it has happened. A very fine couple you both looked in the *Evening Standard* – 'so well suited' were the words that my daily help used. I take it there will be no family celebration, at least I hope not. If there is, please remember I will not willingly sit down with your sister and her husband, although if you insist, and you are quite at liberty to do that, I shall attend and be the very soul of discretion. I am deliriously happy for you, Nephew, I congratulate you, I congratulate your fiancée. Please give my warmest regards to her mother.

Nephew, the girl improves by the day, she has a new happiness. One day perhaps you will meet again. She has become fascinated by the culture of orchids, and I have had built a small glasshouse for her in which to keep the collection. The girl spends hours working at them. They bloom at this time of the year. Our Christmas will be decorated by the most beautiful of blooms, rare blooms in profusion.

Your Uncle

PRIVATE AND TOTALLY CONFIDENTIAL
TO BE OPENED ONLY BY THE ADDRESSEE

Dear Nephew

I write this letter to record a moment in history. I have heard, I will not tell you how, that Indonesia intends to invade Australia. You may find that surprising, yet to the Indonesians it is totally logical, they have for many years regarded Australia as the southern part of their country. They see this great empty land as they sit on their cramped islands. They see its enormous wealth – oil, diamonds, one third of the world's output, iron ore and gold, uranium and the Lord knows what else – not to mention cattle and sheep.

The Australians regard this part of their continent with contempt, and by their actions indicate to others that they have little interest in it. Their armed forces are several days' travel away, their navy a week's sailing, their air force can be there in five hours, as, I may say, given an equal start, can the Indonesian ground forces.

The Australian government has been warned by the Americans. They are not prepared to believe them. Their ambassador in Jakarta is preparing to sign the biggest trade deal in his nation's history, and will hear no evil of the Indonesians. He is wrong, totally wrong. How hard it is to stop once history begins to move.

Nephew, prepare carefully for this event, for it is from such happenings that great reputations are made.

Your Uncle

Dear Nephew

You will have heard this on the news already – 500,000 Indonesians in the night invaded Australia. Not a gun amongst them. They landed where white Australians have never been. They feed like locusts off the native wildlife, they eat food that only Aboriginals would eat, and that coastline can support ten times their number.

What you will not hear or read about is the failure of the Australian air-force transports to land at either Broome or the military strip outside Derby. When they flew in they found both strips covered with squatting Indonesian women and children who were camped there cooking their meal. It was the same at Kununurra. The second wave of Indonesians is at this time landing at Port Hedland. They block the airport both there and at Exmouth. There is not a strip open from Darwin in the north as far south as Meekatharra. The scale of the civilian invasion has completely thrown the Australians and the last reports from the ambassador in Jakarta indicate that 'the trade talks are going extremely well'. He has just received a message of congratulations from his prime minister – all is confusion.

There is to be an emergency debate in the House this afternoon. The government are refusing to support Australia. They will only follow the UN's lead and they will lead nowhere. The complication is that this is not an invasion but a migration.

Your Uncle

Dear Nephew

I enclose a draft of our leader's speech. He is anxious to have your views on it. He will deliver it on television tonight in reply to the Prime Minister's statement. The Indonesians have moved troops on to the mainland of Australia to keep order amongst their own civilians. Our leader has demanded that we put our forces at the disposal of the Australian government. He believes that we owe them that at least. The government prevaricate, this whole affair could bring them down.

This is an issue of principle. It is, as we see it, the invasion of one nation by another. As they see it, it is the occupation of empty land owned by one nation making little use of it by another that desperately needs it. The Indonesians quote only two precedents: the British occupation of Australia, and the American occupation of the western half of their continent. Both areas were sparsely populated, both invaded, and to make matters worse an Aboriginal leader has publicly welcomed the Indonesians as liberators of his land.

Our leader sides with the Australians, saying if Indonesia claims that land, let them do it in the courts. The government, for reasons of convenience, backs the Indonesians and would take over Australia's trade agreement. Our leader bets all on law and order – both domestic and international. All laws must be kept, not just the convenient laws. The weaker members of our party are deeply worried by this commitment to the law. They feel he takes a risk of British troops having to fight in Australia – the irony of it all, when God knows how many of their troops died in Europe.

We shall demand a censure debate. Our leader knows this

is the time to strike, even if he has to drag our faint hearts along by their coat tails.

Your Uncle

Dear Nephew

An election is on. It will be a short campaign and a savage one. Our country is in chaos, the world in turmoil.

May I say, Nephew, your speech on the Indonesian situation was brilliant. There you are, Nephew, already Indonesia has won the war of semantics, we refer to their invasion of Australia as the Indonesian situation. First Australians must share their continent, and then Australians will lose their continent. The word Australian will be consigned to the pages of history.

The irony of it all, dear Nephew, is that, given time, that very same continent under a new name will be predominant in the world. The new America has just discovered itself.

Your Uncle

Dear Nephew

What a campaign – a march to triumph. The lights burn in the office as I write these words, they send out for more champagne. Our leader has just arrived, they cheer him from the Square, they cheer him from every nook and cranny in the building.

A man who a month ago had a problem attracting an audience for his uncomfortable views, whom many regarded as dangerous with his troublesome ideas, is this night a hero.

Nephew, the baggage of an inefficient and weak government once more moves from Downing Street. The age of principle begins. I will not sleep tonight, I doubt if I will sleep for nights to come. My chance has come: in this man, the new prime minister, I can believe.

I am sorry that you cannot be here at the centre of things in our moment of triumph. I have just seen your amazing majority – the largest in the country, many congratulations.

Your Uncle

Dear Nephew

Nephew, I apologize. When I sat down to write it was to congratulate you on your victory. To write to you at some length about it. To offer you some thoughts that might be of use to you. I am afraid, Nephew, I became carried away with my own thoughts and I am certain that when we meet you will tell me that I have got my ideas about life all wrong. You have fought two elections and won both. You see how 'things' are from Westminster, the pinnacle of government. May I point out to you, Nephew, that pinnacles are not the place from which to observe how goes life among the ants.

Well, Nephew, at last, congratulations. A member of the House of Commons and engaged to a girl of good family, happily in possession of a very considerable amount of money, and with real expectations of that sum being quadrupled on the death of her parents. A pretty girl in a country way. I thank you for your hand-written note that arrived first thing on the morning after Polling Day.

Nephew, how your manners have improved since first we spoke of your political career. Do you remember how I admired your rudeness? You are making a conventional marriage that would have pleased your mother and I have no doubt pleases your constituents, and with your new wife's money you will find life easier. Indeed, you could cut a bit of a dash – buy a country house, shoot, summer where the sun really shines, move in a circle much taken with the fun of living.

Nephew, you are tempted. Nurture that strain of hate in your soul lest luxury and good fortune extinguish it. Nephew, do you still wish power, real power, the power to change the lives of the people? Nephew, do you still want office for the purpose of bringing about a better society in our land, or do you want office as a bauble to point at, to top a list of your achievements? Make up your mind, Nephew. Will you be a coward and take the easy route? It's there – little effort, a great deal of holding your tongue and it is all yours. Have I to call you coward? Of course not. I make my judgement, there is steel in you, you have no alternative, I saw it the first day that we spoke. No, Nephew, enjoy your luck, but never cease to dream. Let not the slumber of convenience halt your uneasy dreams.

We will lunch next Thursday at my club. There are many there who will wish to buy you a drink – keep the afternoon free. I fear I have been too busy to spend time with the girl. My new master makes me work late. These are stirring times, so much happens.

Your Uncle

Dear Nephew

I have just spent the day at Chequers. We all lunched together – the PM, his new Cabinet, the Party Chairman and his deputy. The Chairman is not in the Cabinet, the Press are speculating about his disappointment at what appears to be his omission. He has no wish to be in this or any other cabinet, for the simple reason that he would have to resign several lucrative directorships, as well as give up the company car and chauffeur that he enjoys as chairman of an electrical appliance manufacturer, and I suppose a great number of other perks as well. There are those in our office who feel that the Chairman sacrifices the prestige of his office for the sake of his own financial reward. True, a Cabinet minister is poorly paid by the standards that industrialists enjoy, even if they are equipped with a government car and chauffeur, for a government car and chauffeur cannot be used on other than government business, and as the Chairman in the course of his duties engages in Party rather than government business, both car and chauffeur would spend most of their time in the garage.

No, Nephew, this Chairman, who had such an unpromising start, and this PM, who in Opposition few thought would last six months, work well together, their minds are as one mind. They do not need to sit beside each other at a Cabinet table, the one to reassure the other. In the past four years these two men have worked to rebuild the Party, to change it from confusion, a party without principle or ideas. It has been a savage time, Nephew. There are the souls of those cut down who howl in the wilderness, there are those for whom the pace was too hot, who mourn what might have been, those who were inadequate, who whimper of injustice. All their consternation was drowned by the shout of triumph as our

[180]

new party sets out to reform the nation – and reforming our nation does need, for it is in a sorry state after several terms of socialism practised by different parties.

Nephew, when the PM was a backbencher they said he was boring; when he led us in Opposition, they said that he was serious and without humour; as they sat lunching with the PM taking the centre place at the Chequers dining table, they laughed at his jokes. In truth, Nephew, the man is a great wit, and power has made him (for those who seek preferment) the greatest wit. The food at Chequers, I am afraid, has slipped away in quality in tandem with the quality of the governments our nation has suffered under.

What a day that was, Nephew – this May the weather is better than any August's. It's called Chequers weather. We took our coffee on the terrace, the men in shirtsleeves. We sat on the benches in front of the house, the swimming pool to the right of us, and looked over the rose garden, the earliest of the roses just in bloom. Out across the fields with their tenants, the cattle stripping the fresh grass. We looked far across those fields to the Victory Gate built by the order of Churchill in memory of victory in the Second World War. This was the Britain of the past. We now set out to deal with a very different Britain, the Britain of the present, and as we sat we spoke of the Britain of the future.

One by one the PM called the members of his Cabinet to him. They walked among the roses, spoke in quiet voices. On the terrace I sat with their colleagues. We spoke to each of trivialities, of the fine weather. None spoke of the Chequers they knew before, for none of them had known that place. This was a Cabinet without stain, without blemish, untainted by the futile posturing and posing of the past, a Cabinet untouched by failure. This is a right-thinking Cabinet, the PM told me as he chose them. He just rolled the lists that he had been given by well-wishers from the past into paper balls, one after another they flew through the air to end on his office carpet. No cricketer this PM, thank God.

Nephew, he said to me, 'I am a clean-slate man. I want every member of my Cabinet to have a clean slate. It is not flaws in their private lives to which I refer – no, I care little about their private lives. I want purity in their public lives. I want no trace of responsibility for creating unemployment on their hands. I want their consciences clear of involvement with causing industrial disaster. I want them to have played no part in the policies that caused men and women to lose their homes. The Cabinet ministers that I choose must be clear of the guilt of office in a government that so nearly destroyed both our nation and our Party.'

There is no bitterness in this man, just a great determination that humiliations of the past should not be repeated.

Nephew, we took tea in the great hall. They wandered with cake and plate in one hand, weak tea in cup with saucer in the other hand, balancing the two, searching out rooms where history was made and the artefacts of that history. The ring that brought Scotland's kings to rule in England. The table where Napoleon signed his surrender. The portraits of Cromwell and other great men. The lion held in a net painted by Rubens with its mouse added by the brush of Churchill. The stained-glass windows with the arms of past prime ministers, some great, some traitors to that office – these new Cabinet ministers wandered through rooms where cabinets pondered the conduct of wars, studies where prime ministers pondered the affairs of Cabinet ministers. They looked through leaded windows at rolling lawns with woods and hills behind, at avenues and hedges clipped. Slowly, as they absorbed the history of the place, they changed from politicians to become a government, the majesty and the responsibility of their office dawning slowly on them. They were a new Cabinet, new to the ways of Chequers. Only the Party Chairman had been there before, he knew the form.

The Party Chairman spoke. 'Gentlemen, I believe the PM has business to attend to.' So, turning to the Prime Minister, he took him by the hand. 'Thank you, PM, for your hospitality. May I express the feelings of all those present today. We thank you for what you have done for our Party. We wish you well in what you undertake for our nation. We pledge you our loyalty, our time and our energy. May success attend our efforts.'

A few of those present clapped, the Lord Chief Justice intoned, 'Hear, hear,' one or two dabbed tears from their eyes. I noted their names, for it is always those who cry at the congratulations that attend your success who in the end, when times are hard, cry loudest for your resignation. I noted their names, for the Chairman was sure to ask me for them. They all left much as they had come – like a party of day trippers visiting a stately home, looking around for a view not fully taken in before, determined to take value for their entrance money.

The PM took me aside into the white study. We watched the news, recorded earlier, of the pictures of the Cabinet arriving, the live or nearly live pictures of their going. 'A motley crew,' said the PM. It would have been hard not to agree with him about these men and women brought together by a dozen different reasons. They have in common one thing – they seem people of principle, of morality, able to understand the moral dimension of policy. A very dangerous band indeed, for should the PM vary from these policies of principle, should his stance be morally dubious, then he will face practised enemies. I drew his attention to this. 'Every man needs a spur to drive him on. Government is not just about holding office, it is about carrying out the policies that you believe in.' For too long, all government has been a matter of how to trim, how far to trim and to get away with it. Should the PM fail, the Cabinet will drive him on rather than he having to pull the Cabinet after him. They may not be brilliant but, Nephew, they are sound.

The PM poured me a drink of my favourite whisky, you know it well. He told me he wanted a radical government. 'I will announce that we intend to make all cars electric within the next four years. I will announce that we intend to revolutionize the whole of our transport system. We need an integrated transport system. We need a system that improves the quality of life for our nation. We will give grants, huge grants, to the motor companies to develop and produce electric engines. The results of this policy will be, first, a demand for electricity, a demand the electricity companies must prepare to face.

'Secondly, fewer people will use the roads for long-distance travel, for public transport will be quicker and cheaper. We will need fewer roads – this will save the destruction of our landscape, make motoring a pleasurable undertaking.

'Third, we must improve the rail system to make it extremely fast and efficient.'

The PM took a long draft of his whisky. 'What of the motor industry?' I asked him. 'They will be forced to export and, with the help of our grants, to build electric cars. At first, as Britain will be the only country to take this attitude towards motor cars, imports of foreign cars will fall away, and so our balance of payments will improve dramatically.

'This is a moral policy, because it sets out to preserve the quality of life of the population. It is a policy that will not cost a job, because fewer and fewer people are now employed making motor cars. We, the government, will lose the tax on fuel, but this can be replaced by a tax on travel. Industrial goods will still be allowed to travel by lorry where necessary, but those lorries will be electric. There will be no ban on lorries. The railways will be encouraged to compete with road transport and in time they will win. We can build monorails in our cities, rejuvenate the canal systems in our countryside.

Perhaps even coastal shipping will return to our waters, we may in time become again a nation of seamen.'

Nephew, I can tell you this all came as a considerable shock to me, but hardly as great a shock as the PM's next announcement. 'I have had an external working party going into the detail of all this. The Paper will come to the Cabinet in time for Thursday's meeting.' He handed me an envelope. 'In confidence, I will give you a copy of their report.' I have it, Nephew, on my desk as I write. When I sign this letter I shall begin to read it.

Well, Nephew, you no doubt have read this long missive all the time wondering what the PM has in mind for you. I shall not beat about the bush – he intends to make you Financial Secretary at the Treasury. Both he and I hold you in high regard. This letter comes to you by hand so you will, I hope, receive it tonight. I have taken the trouble to find out your whereabouts. You were tactful enough not to hang on the end of a telephone waiting for the PM to call you.

You spend the weekend with your new fiancée. You will marry during the summer recess, perhaps? Her mother should be well pleased with your rise to fame, and you well pleased with your future wife's prospects.

The PM's office will ring tomorrow asking you to call into Downing Street. Congratulations and good luck. Dear Nephew, I would not have asked for more for you. The PM has been extremely generous.

Nephew, I have had little time for the girl recently. She does well. I am consumed with guilt at failing to visit her, but with the election and the excitement of victory I have had no time even for the short trips to Hammersmith. She seems changed in the last few weeks. I hope desperately that she becomes a different person, able to cope with a life bound by conventions. She has missed so much by her past behaviour.

Dear Nephew, we will try to meet later in the week, if only for a drink. I know your life will be hectic for a few months.

Perhaps at my office. I know the Chairman might care to have a few words with you.

Your Uncle

Dear Nephew

I received a call from your private secretary summoning me to see you mid-afternoon on Thursday next. I must decline. I lunch with the PM that day and I expect he will need my presence for most of that afternoon.

May I point out your extreme rudeness in having your minion speak to me in that way – this is not how you treat an uncle, an uncle who has gone to considerable trouble on your behalf often enough. Furthermore, this is not how you should treat one who has the ear of the Prime Minister – not, that is, if you wish to prosper during this government. You might instruct your man on how I should be treated properly. I shall expect a note of apology. The Chairman incidentally is very put out that you did not come and see him.

> *Your Uncle*

PS A letter of apology to the Chairman as well would not go amiss.

Dear Nephew

The Chairman was delighted to receive your note. He is of the opinion that it would be helpful for the two of you to meet and suggests lunch at White's. This can only be to your advantage, for a good class of gossip will see you sit down to eat with the Party Chairman. This, as well as your well known friendship with the Prime Minister, will set you on the road to being considered a person of great influence.

You will be told stories by those who seek to please you in order one day to solicit your assistance. You will be asked favours by those who need them and have a less subtle turn of mind. These favours, Nephew, will tell stories of their own. Put one with another, and soon you will be one of the best informed men in the land. Do not give this information to my Chairman, however charming he may be, and regardless of how much you desire to do him a favour to repay his hospitality and charm. In the world of politics information is a currency. It should be spent sparingly – tell only a little at a time, then tell it where it can have most effect.

Nephew, just a word of advice when you fix the luncheon appointment with my Chairman. Telephone his secretary yourself. I know you would normally ask your girl to ring her, on this occasion do it yourself. There are two reasons for this. The first is that, it being unusual for you to arrange luncheon appointments yourself, the civil servants will consider your lunching with my Chairman as a matter of greater significance than it really is. This will ensure their telling colleagues in other ministries and those colleagues telling their ministers. If you wish an event to be published in the most effective way, by word of mouth is a means well worth using, all believing only a few know of the event but in reality all knowing of the event, then make that event appear to be out of the ordinary. If you wish discretion, make that event appear so ordinary that it becomes boring.

One lunch arranged with my Chairman by yourself is news. Regular lunches fixed by your secretary are, to those who listen for news, pure tedium. If you wish a lunch to go unremarked, fix a series of them, and after the first do not bother with the next but, as each appointment approaches, cancel it for some mundane reason. A dentist, perhaps – that excuse has worked before.

The second reason is that the secretary to my Chairman is a most powerful woman with a memory filled to the brim with information about the past; she sees all. No matter of consequence passes through that office without her knowing. Even when information is so secret that it is hidden from her, those who hide the information do not seem to realize that this woman knows so much of the framework of life in our office that she can guess with considerable accuracy the secrets they hide. The very act of hiding information alerts her to its existence. She will be flattered if you telephone her yourself, and do flatter her, Nephew, take trouble to make her your friend, for the higher that you rise in life the more you have need of friends at life's roots. This woman, who has passed you your tea as you sat at meetings in the office, is a woman who can influence events far greater than you might expect from her status. Nephew, make her your friend, do not hesitate, because you do not fully understand the role of those who assist.

You wrote to me, Nephew. I am grateful for your words of apology. I take them as an apology, though in truth they had all the makings of an excuse. An excuse coupled with a complaint. You wrote to me complaining about the way your policy paper on law and order is to be implemented. You complain that the guts have been torn out of it. I smiled as I read that, and then laughed out loud as I read that you had telephoned the Prime Minister to put him right on this matter.

He was pleased that you took the trouble to telephone him. He complimented you on the way you set out your case, he told you that you had convinced him. You were flattered that he listened to you for over forty-five minutes. How I laughed when you ended by telling me that the Home Office still took little notice of your arguments and went their own sweet way. Double-faced, you called our Prime Minister – that and a dozen other names.

I have burned your letter. I suggest that you do the same with mine. Nephew, never, never telephone prime ministers. Never discuss more than their health with them if they telephone you. Civil servants listen carefully to all you say, and before you went to bed that night the arguments in favour of your policy were sitting neatly typed on the desk of a civil servant at the Home Office whose job it was to prepare a brief that would destroy each and every one of those arguments when it was raised with the Home Secretary by the Prime Minister. You exposed your hand and it was cut off. I am afraid we will have to start again. Call by my office next Tuesday. I have something of an idea that could help you.

Nephew, you were unwise when you rang the PM to talk about law and order, downright foolish when you suggested that the PM's Press secretary was responsible for the adverse publicity that our policies are getting. You are right, of course. He is a lout of a man who would not know a philosophy if it were written in capital letters using words of fewer than five letters and then held in front of his eyes. As for the Party, he has played no part in it, knows nothing of it, has total contempt for it and wrongly imagines that it does not matter. Substitute his name for the word Party and you have here roughly the Party's feeling about him. One day he will bring the PM down, but he will not be dismissed, not now, not ever.

You, Nephew, have made a powerful enemy. Keep out of his way and hope that he forgets your ill advised conversation. I doubt if he will, but let us for the moment go forward with that hope.

Nephew, we must get that policy in place, it is important for our party and our nation. I have spoken with the PM. He agrees that at present we must not lose the Home Secretary, the wettest member of the Cabinet, put there in a job that destroys. He will in time be destroyed, but by his own hand not ours. The implementing of these policies needs careful timing.

You, Nephew, have a lot to learn about negotiation, and in government much is negotiation so you must learn speedily. Never go into a negotiation with rigid aims fuelled by enthusiasm; indifference is the way to success when negotiating. Let your opponents know that you do not care the slightest about the outcome. Time is important: do not allow your opponents to believe you to have a deadline, take the attitude that you are prepared to spend the rest of your life talking, if you have points to give, give them up quickly, then settle down to destroying your opponent's arguments, argument after argument. Put aside conceit, pride and arrogance, and if you cannot put them aside, hide them, forget the vanity of victory. You wish to implement a policy because that policy is right, not because you wish to be proven right.

In the end, Nephew, it all comes down to stamina. Do not give up, little by little we will have our policy, in the end, for the moment we must argue.

Write soon, Nephew, I enjoy your letters and, despite all those around me, I find myself a lonely man. Your sister is as ill behaved as she is ugly. If she wishes a house of a larger size, then her husband must provide it; if she wishes funds further than the not inconsiderable ones that her father left her, then her tedious husband must provide those also. What does that most tiresome of men do for a living? Import, export, insurance, stockbroking or something in the City, perhaps he is a merchant banker, I do not care for any of those trades. Is he self-employed, or perhaps he is employed managing your sister's funds – surely he can't live on his parliamentary salary? Why does this wretched sister of yours, whom I dislike so much, continue to pester me with invitations, invitations to entertain her and her brute to expensive meals, when to see how that man leaves stains on his claret glass makes me vomit. How can such a tedious little man always be so accurate with his political predictions? Who on earth tells him of these matters? I am certain others to whom he tells his tales believe that he gets his information from me.

Nephew, I have to see your sister, for curiosity as to that man's next political scenario consumes me. I hate them both but I cannot break free from the total accuracy of his views.

God bless you, Nephew.

Your loving Uncle

PS I have sent by hand to your ministry a set of documents that I would value your opinion on. Do not hurry to return them, they are not urgent, but we must get this matter right. Discuss it if you will with your adviser. The PM has approved your seeing these papers. They are, of course, extremely confidential. Lock them in a safe place.

Dear Nephew

I was greatly taken with your description of the row
between you and the Home Secretary. I wish that I had been
present as a witness. The whole episode sounds the greatest
of fun. There is, Nephew, no form of entertainment half as
pleasurable as a good row between colleagues. Do not,
Nephew, take these interludes with any seriousness. The
Home Secretary will not destroy your credit, or for that
matter you his. Political wars go on until peace breaks out,
and no one really knows how they start or why they end. The
issues that politicians fight over are seldom the reason for a
war. Their actions as recorded by historians are often misin-
terpreted. Take the case of the defence secretary who, in a
row over the ownership of a supplier of armaments, left the
Cabinet room. His colleagues thought that he went to relieve
himself, in fact he left to resign. Could he not have done that
then and there? Of course, he could have resigned to the
Cabinet as a whole, or to the Prime Minister in private. His
colleagues believed that he addressed his resignation to the
waiting Press for maximum effect. Perhaps that was so. He
may, however, have feared that his colleagues would have
persuaded him to stay, giving in on the issue that he fought
for. The Prime Minister might even have offered him an alternative job to keep him in the government. Fear forced his
resignation in this manner – fear that he might go back on a
decision to resign. The issue was of little importance, the
presence of the Press far from accidental, the action premedi-
tated and planned long before.

Nephew, reflect carefully before coming to conclusions
about men and women from words written about them. As
for your row with the Home Secretary, it is of no consequence. When he needs your help, you will become his friend.

Political careers are ruined by politicians themselves, and political careers are likewise made by the efforts of the man or woman concerned. Others play only a small part in the fate of a politician, although it would seem otherwise.

Your Uncle

Dear Nephew

Congratulations on your marriage. I enjoyed the ceremony more than I can say. All is as I had always hoped. You hold high office with the prospect of higher. You have made an advantageous marriage. All and sundry speak well of you.

Nephew, I should end this letter here for I have so far only good thoughts of you. I cannot, but I do not wish you to construe what I have now to write as gratuitous criticism. Your friends, Nephew – you have too many of them and they are of the wrong kind. I never hear that you plot and plan, no, you are too well taught, too clever by far to be caught at that. However, I know you as you know me; each of us has our weaknesses and each of us has our strengths. You have a desire to have men like you, I am indifferent as to how they think of me. In you I perceive an ability to suit your actions to your conscience, for myself my actions are judged by my conscience. Remember, Nephew, do not incur debts that cannot in good conscience be repaid.

We together have set out on a path of principle, we have both espoused hard policies. You approach your first Budget. You for the first time in your life have real power, the power to make friends, the power to make enemies. Do not, Nephew, fall into the temptation of using this power for your political advantage. Consider why you need political success – only to implement the policies that you believe in. If during the journey to political success you have to cast overboard the baggage of conscience, then what, Nephew, is the point of that journey?

Your Uncle

Dear Nephew

The Budget that your master constructed was well received. I know that you handed him the tools for his job. I pray that you did not pay a price for them. I fear that you may have.

Nephew, I have news privately that the Foreign Secretary is seriously ill. I expect him to inform the Prime Minister of this at the weekend. He is invited to Chequers. I will be staying there also, and I have put it in the Prime Minister's mind that you should go to the Foreign Office. I pointed out to him how perceptive you were in the matter of the Indonesian affair. He has taken the point and speaks about you being the next Foreign Secretary. He does not know how soon this will be.

The PM was extremely impressed by your handling of the Budget negotiations. All parties seemed to have come out of them with a feeling of well being.

Negotiation is the art of making events possible. Governing is totally different. Governing is about making events happen. Simply, it is called leading. Negotiation must with equal simplicity be called housekeeping. Budgets should be the consequence of government, so often government is the consequence of a Budget.

The rare orchids bloom. The girl prospers. I am in the confidence of the PM. All is well.

Your Uncle

BY HAND
URGENT AND PRIVATE

Dear Nephew

The Foreign Secretary's resignation is on the PM's desk. The Chief Whip comes to see him this afternoon. I have spoken to the Chief Whip, you are our candidate, good luck, Nephew.

Your Uncle

BY HAND

Dear Nephew

A note scribbled in haste. I'm afraid that we failed. Another
is to go to the Foreign Office. You, however, are to join the
Cabinet as Chief Secretary at the Treasury.

Your Uncle

Dear Nephew

Just a note to formally congratulate you on your elevation to Chief Secretary.

I am certain that a man of your capability will come to terms with the job in a short time.

Nephew, I am still worried about your friendships, they seem to me to be altogether too casual for your own good. The Chief Whip used the words 'universally liked'. The PM spoke of the regard in which you are held by his critics, phrases like 'he spans the divide in our Party', 'a healer', 'a conciliator' are often attached to your name.

Nephew, the man who stands in the middle of the road sooner or later gets run down.

Your Uncle

PS Your sister insists on seeing me. I suppose that she is after a position for her detestable husband. I wish him eternal life on the back benches. There is this time much that I could do to help that man, Nephew, there is nothing that I will do. Do not deal with this fellow or his emissary, your sister. She is bad, bad, bad.

Dear Nephew

How is your wife? Is she in good health? Fully recovered from the birth of your son? How your mother would have been filled with joy. I am sad that she missed the birth of the heir to our family name, but there it is, we all miss her, a fine woman but not a woman of any strength of character.

I am truly delighted in your son, his birth seems to have given me a new lease of life. I cannot tell you of the excitement that I felt when I heard it was a boy.

I was extremely upset by your sister's remarks. I believe that wretched sister of yours was quite unfair. The house should be yours, it has been in your family for generations and I hope there it remains. I cannot accept your invitation to stay. I cannot leave the girl at weekends, I must spend those with her. I long to spend my time with her. I take it that she would not be a welcome guest. Ah well, you set your course and I set mine.

Your Uncle

Dear Nephew

Your sister is deeply jealous of you, she is possibly your only enemy, she makes that quite clear and she wishes to be bought. Her price — a senior position for her husband. I advise you do not give this woman anything. She cannot be bought, whatever she may say. She is a woman whose price cannot be paid. She has no intention to settle. The solution to this problem I will reflect on.

Meanwhile to business. The PM intends to take a drastic course with the Irish.

I warn you that his course of action will be hotly opposed by your department. They will say to you that this course of action will destroy the European Community. Do not, Nephew, use this as a reason to oppose his policy, for it is this very aspect that commends the policy to him.

Your Uncle

Dear Nephew

Our Prime Minister comes more and more at odds with his Cabinet. He must make changes, make changes now, for a Cabinet is like a team of horses, and the Prime Minister its coachman. They must be carefully balanced. One member that would run wild is no use in a Cabinet. The Prime Minister must drive them forward, or hold them back, turn them to the right or the left, he cannot pull the coach himself, nor should he try, and without a strong coachman the horses would all pull in different directions. The Prime Minister sets the tone and the pace of his government more than any other, giving that government its direction. But in the end it is the partnership of horses and coachman that moves the coach.

Nephew, keep clear of these plotters who abound in our government. To change this leader would be a terrible mistake. His problems can be resolved. He must depend more on his Party, less on his civil servants. He must remember where he came from and ensure that he has support in the constituencies. Remove him, and the anger of the Party's activists will smoulder long after he is gone – why? Not because they love him, they love any leader; rather because you and your colleagues in Parliament have removed him without reference to them. Succeed and, for a while, his successor will survive; fail and any member of this new leader's government who shows a hint of failure, both personal or professional, will be torn to shreds. The Party's activists will have then their revenge, for a long forgotten slight.

Nephew, rumour, who is a lying jade, has it that you might stand against him. Pull back, Nephew, control your greed. You have come a long way very fast – take time, play a long game. Let others wield the knife and take its murderous reward. Wait in the distance. Wait and you will win all.

Your Uncle

Dear Nephew

Our Prime Minister sinks further and further into his bunker, with no support for his policies. Now he blames his ministers' lack of ability in explaining these policies. So as his followers clearly cannot explain the policies, the Prime Minister takes the view that they need no explanation and so sets out to push them through regardless. It is all a tragedy, for the man is a genius – beset by a bunch of mindless opportunists. Mindless, I am wrong in that, for they have minds, cunning minds, your friends bite at the ankles, never daring to strike at the throat.

Nephew, dragons in shallow water were ever the sport of shrimps. Never was this so true. This man, our Prime Minister, has grand ideas, ideas that would greatly benefit our nation. But the political climate is wrong for these ideas, the timing is wrong, the people that he has to work with are the wrong people. Once again, politics destroys the vision of a great man. A great leader, it is not that he lacks the ability to inspire others with his ideas, just that those charged with carrying them out fear for their futures. They flee to the comfort of smaller, safer policies. They like the trappings of office and intend to keep them.

Your Uncle

Dear Nephew

I know that there is a strong feeling among your colleagues that the Prime Minister has gone too far. This Ireland Bill must first face the test of public opinion. The Prime Minister is not prepared to do that – he will have his Bill, or call an election. You wrote to me asking my opinion on this matter. Uncharacteristic of you to write such a letter when we could so easily meet to discuss the whole issue. I assume, therefore, that my reply is to be read by others, so, suspecting this, I reply thus:

I am totally behind the Prime Minister in this matter. He is a good man who needs the support of his colleagues to carry out a seemingly unpopular policy. In the matter of your suggestion that he could call an election which we would in all probability lose, I do not fear this, for prime ministers do not call elections, the Monarch does, and if the Prime Minister should resign, the Monarch will ask another member of our party to form a government. We have, after all, a sizeable majority, and this government still has time to run.

A prime minister can only resign his own position. Nephew, if as you indicate there is a strong body of opinion in the Cabinet against him, the election of a new leader who can command a majority in the House should present no problem. The Monarch will be so advised, and will take that course. If you are wrong, however, your fate will lie with the electorate.

Nephew, the Prime Minister does not deserve this treatment. I must tell you that I will not be a party to it. I am his friend and his man. I will fight alongside him.

Your Uncle

Dear Nephew

Disaster has struck. Your sister visited the girl while she was alone. She took with her those two harridans who I had hoped were part of a sad tale long past. How she met the messenger and her companions I do not know. Perhaps she always knew of them and of my affairs with that pair. There was a scene. I shudder to think of the form that it took. The outcome – the girl left home and by nightfall was to be found in the intensive care unit of a London hospital. Your sister has told the Press of my relationship with her. I have had them on my neck non-stop all day.

You were right, Nephew, in the course of action that you took. I have over the years found fault with your attitude to the girl and over the years forgiven you for it. I understand now that you are only a politician, as people perceive politicians. You use guile but have not heart. You have never understood when I wrote and warned you that if you will truly succeed, you and your work must be one. If you have not honesty, humanity and a love of the rightness of life, then you may with trickery succeed, but your success will be the most awful of failures.

Now simply put out a statement that the girl was your adopted sister who left home many years ago. You have not seen her since then, you are sorry for her state as you would be sorry for any young woman in that state. Let it be known that, should any try to damage your reputation through the use of her story, you will sue and sue again.

Nephew, your sister has had her day of spite.

Your Uncle

BY HAND – URGENT
PRIVATE AND CONFIDENTIAL

Dear Nephew

This afternoon I was taken for questioning by the police – I do not know what the outcome of all this will be. I have sent my resignation to the PM. I do not expect an exchange of letters. I have apologized for the embarrassment that I have caused him.

I am too tired by my experience to write at length. I shall sleep now and call you in the morning,

Your Uncle

PRIVATE AND CONFIDENTIAL
BY HAND
TO BE OPENED BY ADDRESSEE ONLY

Dear Nephew

I rang your office this morning. Your secretary told me that you were involved in meetings for most of the day. She was pleasant, as she usually is, and promised faithfully to have you call me when you had a free moment. It seems, Nephew, that you did not have such a moment.

I understand your position and I write only to set out mine. First the matter of the girl. She has been arrested for soliciting, and will appear before the magistrate and receive a small fine. Your sister and her friend are behind this. I have experienced police questioning under caution, and I may well be charged. When, one year later, I am acquitted I will have suffered considerable expense and the destruction of my career. In all probability you already know of my plight in some detail. Nevertheless, I shall write of it for you.

This time Saturday morning I was at Hammersmith working on my papers when the police arrived, a tall detective chief inspector and a smooth youthful assistant. The girl shows them into the house and without much ado they arrest her. A female police officer takes her away in a police car, while the senior officer and his assistant question me. I must come with them to Tottenham Court Road police station, I am likely to be charged with a criminal offence. 'What offence?' I ask. That, they say, can wait till later. I ask for and receive permission to call my lawyer, our family lawyer, he will meet me at their station.

We – the two policemen, their driver and myself – travel to London in silence. I am shown into a room twice as tall as it is wide or long. One window high in a wall, a window made of heavy glass blocks that admit neither light nor air; two doors, one through which we entered, the other leads, I suppose, to the cells. That room stank with months of accumulated fear, the vomit of prisoners and the sweat of their interrogators. My family solicitor sat on a small chair against the wall, I across a table from the two police officers. My solicitor offered little help for he has no criminal experience, his only contribution was to confirm that some time ago a government abolished the right of a suspect to remain silent, should I say nothing it could be used against me at my trial. The junior police officer explained the workings of his tape recorder and the procedure for taking a statement, then they both began to question me. They sneered at me with their politeness, they intimidated me with their manners. After two hours I would have agreed to plead guilty to any crime, just to get out of that place. I answered their questions as best I could, for I knew little, they seemed to know all. I am accused of living off immoral earnings, my source of income the girl.

I was released into the night – you can read of my plight in most of today's newspapers, for photographers were at the police station and the time of my release was convenient to the deadline of their journals. There you have it, Nephew, my reputation already half destroyed. I am warned that I will probably be charged, at which time what fragments of reputation I still have will be scattered to the four winds. I will wait one year at least before my trial and an opportunity to show all of this accusation to be lies.

Nephew, you are famous for your policy on law and order, you hold high office and, with that office, responsibility. Nephew, you know nothing of the law. You may dine with judges, drink at the bar of the Garrick Club with lawyers, but you know nothing of the reality of the law and its danger to the innocent. Far better ten criminals go free than one innocent man or woman be wrongfully committed. The right to silence must be restored. You are with great speed taking away one by one the protections that are the citizen's right, and the reason that you give for taking these protections is

that they are an encumbrance on the police in the perform-
ance of their duty, the duty to convict the guilty at any cost.

Your Uncle

Dear Nephew

I still wait for your letter.

I have, as you will have read, been charged with the criminal offence of living off immoral earnings. I paid the girl's fine and we live in the same house.

Life goes on here, a rhythm of boredom beaten out by days that lack all interest. I read the newspapers. I care little for what they say. I long to live abroad, but most I long for employment. Have you the position of consul open somewhere? I suppose the accusation of a crime bars me from such a position. The scandal is over, it lasted barely a day. There is nothing more to be said. When I am tried all will see my innocence, but it all takes so long.

Nephew, I have not seen you for some time, or so it seems. We must get together. There is still advice that I need to give you. I am worried about that Irish Bill, I have read nothing of it in the Press.

My best wishes to your wife and son. How is the boy? God bless him.

Your Uncle

PRIVATE AND CONFIDENTIAL
BY HAND
TO BE OPENED BY ADDRESSEE ONLY

Dear Nephew

Why do you not call? Why can you not come to my house at Hammersmith? You keep yourself from me and I am kept from the PM when he needs my support the most. I have read about the problems that he has with the Irish Bill, about the rebellions that are threatened; I have read between the lines, and I read of plots. Your name is the name that leads these plotters. You are much talked of as the new Prime Minister, the words that are used say this. 'The Prime Minister is too uncompromising for our times, the electorate wish to have a sensible touch at the helm of government, without doubt the electorate favour a conciliator as prime minister.' Nephew, without a shadow of doubt you and your friends set out to destroy a great and honest man. Were I not under the shadow of shame I would put you all about your business. I sit in loneliness at my house in Hammersmith and I wonder how it is that I am excluded from the political battle at this time; and as I wonder I reflect on this happy coincidence for you and your friends. What is the truth of the matter?

Your Uncle

Dear Nephew

Perhaps I wrote too harshly in my last letter. I feel persecuted and that affects my judgement.

I read in the newspapers of the election. I am not surprised that Parliament will not back the PM on his Irish policy. Perhaps he stretched too far. All is not lost. Now it is up to the electorate – the PM always had great faith in the electorate. He set great store by its common sense, a common sense seldom articulated except at elections and times of national crisis.

Sadly, the polls do not reflect his faith. The electorate are asked to speak and who knows the answer? I await it with not a great deal of hope.

When can we have a meal together? In private, of course. I have resigned from my clubs but I still have the flat in Westminster. Perhaps we could dine there. I am available at your convenience. I have no other appointments. Life is a tightrope, Nephew. As we walk it we sway from side to side, all that is needed is for someone to give us a nudge at the wrong moment, not a push, not a shove, just the gentlest of nudges, then we fall, and the higher the tightrope that we walk, the worse the damage of that gentle nudge. I, Nephew, have recently felt that gentle nudge and I have fallen from the game of politics. I do not yet know who nudged me, but I now suspect why I was nudged and I suppose in time I will learn the whole truth of the matter.

Your Uncle

Dear Nephew

Since you will not see me, nor speak to me on the telephone, I am forced to write. You will no doubt notice that I
did not mark this letter private, as is my habit these days. I am
glad this letter was opened by some junior official, for I wish
all to know how you plotted secretly over many years against
the man who gave you advancement in your political career –
the Prime Minister. Not to mention your uncle who, it seems,
wasted much good advice on you.

You, Nephew, with your friends, have moved fast to
dismiss a prime minister just before an election campaign
begins. This is unheard of, but you and your friends have
done just that, attacking the Prime Minister at his weakest
moment, a time when, as a man of honour, finding that
he has little support in his Cabinet, the only road that he
can take is the one to resignation. How right you were –
the whole plot is now revealed, each actor playing his
part to perfection, the right words at the right time. The
Prime Minister has resigned and I am told that by tomorrow
you will lead our party, to victory you believe. The Irish
policy is suppressed, the European Union reinforced,
every sin of this government blamed on the PM, every triumph
yours.

As for myself, my career is over. My life changed from
triumph to ignominy. Nephew, I know your weapons that are
forged to hurt me, and I know that chief amongst them is my
own pride – that is why I took my troubles with the law so
hard. My vanity was hurt and so I misjudged my course of
action. Vanity, Nephew, has brought down far greater men
than me. Beware, Nephew, of vanity, all is vanity, one day
someone may make your vanity the vehicle for your own

downfall. Nephew, I call you traitor and as I say that I feel sorrow for you.

Your Uncle

Dear Nephew

Thank you so much for your communication, the letter
from your secretary. I of all people know you are busy with
the election. I quite understand that you cannot dine even
privately with me at this time – that is the advice I would give
you. I wonder if you even read my letter to you. The tone of
yours leads me to believe that you did not.

Nephew, you always believed that a civil answer turned
away anger. You are right, of course, we all waste so much
time refighting battles long fought. I hope that the PM is as
forgiving as I am. Why, Nephew, did you have to live this life
of treachery, when all you ever required was given to you?

Your Uncle

Dear Nephew

I cannot congratulate you on becoming leader of your party. Forgive, perhaps; congratulate you on your treachery, never. I see that your brother-in-law has become your trusted confidant. Beware that man's wife, for she will have your job for him if she can.

Your Uncle

Dear Nephew

It may seem strange to write and tell you that I spent part of this week with your predecessor. He is like a man who is dead but still he did not forget me.

We attended a service on Sunday near his home and afterwards stood in the small yard of that Staffordshire church. A church in a village where the last Royalists held out against the forces of Parliament. How strange, when he fought all of his life for the tomorrow of our Parliament. Perhaps there was mist by mid-afternoon that day, and I suppose the local pub sells warm beer. As he stood and talked to the group gathered around him (he explained to his constituents that he would not stand for election), it was all so typical of the England of the imagination.

He, however, is a very different man from all that. It is not how matters looked that concern him, not how they seem, rather how they are. He is a man who believes that an honest man begets honesty, an honest family, an honest village, an honest country and so an honest world. This man believed in the strength that honesty gives and the rewards that flow from it. He saw honesty as the best road to fame and fortune, even if that fame was only spiritual and fortune the same. Chicanery and devious devices, plots and plans he saw only as a diversion and as a delay. I sat and talked with him – I, a man accused of crime, who believed my life to be a failure. He appeared to have failed yet I knew with certainty of his success.

He was a man to be followed, whom all followed on the path to success, but when the road to success meant passing across the chasm of failure he walked it alone. Now he is dismissed and this afternoon we sat in his garden and spoke of flowers and agriculture. A change in life, he said, is a time to be taken seriously, not wasted. When you are cast out, that is a time to think, to plan, to prepare. The very words that I should have said to him, crippled by the criminal charge that has struck at the very heart of my self-respect. The memorial to his term of office will be as grand as his dismissal was modest. I expect that you and the others will be quick to offer him reward – after all, the election over, that is the time when you can honour him, raise him up just to be able to point at him should events prove adverse, buy his silence with a non-existent promotion. You fools, so clever in your folly.

Your Uncle

Dear Nephew

Now you lead our Party and by the look of the opinion polls are set fair to becoming prime minister.

After many years of holding your tongue, keeping your opinions only amongst those friends of yours, you have the position that you sought, and have cleverly made it appear that you obtained your position through the popular acclaim of your colleagues. I hope that popularity will not bind your soul once you rule.

The election will be over in ten days, we have no reason to meet. This letter needs no reply, the time for replies is long past.

Your Uncle

Dear Nephew

I cannot congratulate you. How can I not have seen that I was after all just a pawn in a great game? And you, whom I sought to teach, moved me from square to square, and then I was sacrificed so that an attack on the white King could be opened.

Your Uncle

Dear Nephew

You have consistently refused to accept all forms of communication from me – no matter, I send you this letter not so much in the hope that you will read it, rather to make my views a matter of record. I have, Nephew, over many years given you so much advice and guidance, in fact, it could at one time have been said that you were my creature. You for your part prospered by my assistance and for a time seemed to take my advice. How our situations have changed. I am old and disgraced, you are now in charge of the affairs of our nation. The irony of this situation is that I have dealt honourably in the matter of a youthful indiscretion, while you have plotted with your so-called friends to bring down a decent man. You have success, I the bitter food of failure. You, as is your privilege, have amputated my existence from your life. I sought only to help you to success, a success gained honourably, not by a sleight of hand, as you have gained what your admirers call success, your 'friends' call power, and I call dishonour.

Harsh words, my Nephew, they are meant to be. Considering our relative position it may occur to you that any further advice from me can only be worthless. Nephew, I put this proposition to you. 'Whose advice on avoiding the pitfalls that lead to failure is worth the more? The advice of one who has only known success, or the advice of one who has had practical experience of failure?' Your friends, Nephew, have put you in power and they will pull the strings of that power. You, Nephew, are their puppet; you, Nephew, are a member of their club, bound by the morality of that club, each man to do as he pleases, each man supported by his fellow members until he becomes a necessary sacrifice to safeguard the existence of that club. You, Nephew, will appear to lead – in fact you are a follower, a follower of the herd that is your Cabinet, a follower of events, a follower of the whim of each and every editor in Fleet Street. Following all, pleasing none, in time you will go, remembered only for the price of your failure.

Nephew, do not trust those who put you in power. Tomorrow you must announce your Cabinet. Do away with these friends, send them to the back benches. Their only competence is that of intrigue, a contagious disease, once caught never shaken off. Send them to the back benches to plot and plan.

With love
Your Uncle

Dear Nephew

It is with sadness I write to you. I have read the list of your Cabinet, I have read the list of your Ministry. I can only tell you that those lists are but part of the price that you have paid for power. A price which you will pass on to the people of our country. The willing victims of every incompetent administration that ever struggles to power.

Nephew, there is more to say. First, let me inform you that I have called you seven times and sent fifteen separate notes asking you to telephone me. I am informed, I still have some contacts, that you have received each and every one of these and passed them straight to your waste bin, ignoring them as you have my calls.

Secondly, I regard it as an act of treason for your government to abandon the Irish Bill. You worked with your predecessor closely, you gave no indication that you disagreed with his philosophies. Indeed, you rode to power on them.

I can understand, though I hate it, your rejection of me, but I am confounded by your rejection of him and all that he stood for. I believed you to be a man of principle. A man who would search deeply for the moral basis of a policy and, finding that, construct a policy and carry it to its conclusion. You are not such a man.

Your involvement in the destruction of my reputation with your enthusiastic aide, your sister, I can only guess at, as I can only guess the role that you played in the downfall of the Prime Minister. Nephew, when I wrote previously I used the analogy of a chess game. Remember, Nephew, there are other queens and kings, knights and bishops, not to mention a whole host of pawns waiting to assail you.

For me, however, you have never existed. You I would not

follow to water in a desert. You are only the fiction of my own conceit.

I was your uncle